GETTING UNDER HER *Skin*

JACQUELINE HAYLEY

www.jacquelinehayley.com

First edition June 2019

Editing by Sarah Proulx Calfee
www.threelittlewordsediting.com

Proof reading by Kym Mirabito

Cover design by Alyssa Garcia
www.uplifting-designs.com

ISBN: 978-0-6485858-1-7

www.jacquelinehayley.com

To all those girls
with purple hair.

CHAPTER 1

"Darling, you know I'm so proud of your career, but I just had lunch with Darla and she said she'd listened to some podcast-thingy of yours. She was shocked, to be honest."

Oh fuck. Sara Morrison gripped her mobile phone tighter. She totally knew where this was going. And really, it had only been a matter of time before someone had made her mother aware of that particular podcast. Darla Simmons would have delighted in being the one to do so, all the while professing her deepest sympathy and concern for Sara's reputation.

If her mother knew she was standing outside a tattoo studio right now for an interview, she'd need her facial botox topped up immediately.

"You were getting waxed," Teresa continued, "*down there*, and she said it was quite graphic. I knew you didn't just write nice little pieces about Elizabeth Arden lipstick, but it seems like maybe this was, well, going a little too far, frankly. You don't want people to start talking, do you? Especially now that you're seeing Phil – you don't want to jeopardise your relationship by exposing yourself like that."

Sara muffled a sigh. Her parents were by and large supportive of her career choice as beauty editor for the fashion magazine *High Gloss*, but she knew they wouldn't blink twice if she married and gave up her job to be a wife and mother. Hell, they expected that, even though she was only 24-years old. Sara wasn't quite sure if her own desire to get married was just a reflection of theirs, and to be honest, she wasn't prepared to look too closely into it. Phil ticked all the right boxes. Except, maybe, for giving her any kind of shivery feelings. But, she reminded herself, they were the stuff of romance novels, not real life.

"Mum, it wasn't that bad. And honestly, Darla isn't exactly the target demographic we were aiming for with that piece."

Sara needed to distract her mother, before she brought her father into the conversation…

"Imagine what your father would say if he knew this is what you were doing with that journalism degree he paid for."

Oh my god.

"Mother, you paid my rent while I was at college – you didn't pay my course fees. I got a scholarship, remember? You make it sound like I didn't earn my degree. And I can't discuss this with you now, because I'm about to do an interview. For my job. So I'll talk to you later. Bye."

She knew that hanging up like that meant she'd have to visit over the weekend to placate her mother – preferably with flowers.

Her job was one area of her life where Sara was free of parental expectations. They didn't feel the need to interfere in something they believed would be short lived. And with time running out to have a career before she married, Sara was desperate to make her mark. Getting a tattoo, however, was maybe going too far.

At last week's editorial meeting, Bridgette, her editor, had given her the opportunity to do a feature on tattoo artist Mitch Smith. Having recently returned from LA, the Aussie-born tattooist had impressive credentials and a swag of celebrity clients singing his praises.

If Sara had to write one more fluff piece waxing lyrical about the perfect shade of blush, she was going to get stabby – she was getting desperate to write something with a little more substance. But writing about an inked, probably uncouth, tattooist wasn't really what she had in mind.

Unfortunately, the celebrity angle appealed to Bridgette. And then Pauline, the heavily pregnant deputy editor, had goaded Sara into actually getting a tattoo, claiming it would add authenticity to the article. Sara was swayed when Pauline proposed the feature could dovetail nicely into a series of syndicated blog posts, giving Sara more coverage.

That, and the fact that Pauline had made an on-the-quiet recommendation for Sara to be her replacement when she left on maternity leave, sealed the deal.

So here she was in the back of a taxi, having sold her soul for the chance at a career promotion and delaying the inevitable.

"Are you getting out love? This is it, PACIFIC at 180 Campbell Parade," said the elderly cab driver, glancing over his shoulder at her for the second time. She really needed to pay him and get out.

"I know. I live here. In Bondi, I mean," she stalled.

"Right." The driver clearly did not care and was already responding to a radio call about his next fare.

Sighing, Sara paid for the ride with a cab charge supplied by the publishing company and stepped into the late afternoon sunshine, careful to avoid a crowd of loitering teenage hipsters, distracted from their destination by the façade of the newly opened Ink Inc. The level of interest wasn't surprising given the buzz the business had been generating.

Living in Bondi, Sara had watched as the historic Swiss Grand Hotel had undergone a massive redevelopment into PACIFIC, which was now super luxe apartments and a world-class dining and retail precinct, including Ink Inc.

With a prime beachfront location and an industrial Brooklyn vibe, Mitch Smith's tattoo studio looked the goods. As apprehensive as she was about this interview, Sara was equally as intrigued to meet the man behind the ink. She'd done her homework, and the man she'd found online was smoking hot. *Smoking* hot.

It was little wonder that most of the paparazzi-style images had gorgeous women hanging off his arms; his reputation as a charismatic bad boy was well documented.

Realising she was now loitering herself, she rubbed her freshly glossed lips together and straightened her pencil skirt. She looked sharp, and knew it.

It was game time.

Stepping into Ink Inc. she was immediately arrested by a wall of street art – graphic and intricate. It was painted over the exposed brick wall behind the concrete counter top that a served as a front desk, and was a focal point for the raw but sophisticated interior. *High Gloss'* sister publication *High Interiors* would cream their panties over the design of the space, which was uber cool while still boasting a laidback vibe.

The woman behind the counter looked like a 1950s pinup girl, complete with beauty mark sitting just above pouty lips, sailor tat on her arm and an hourglass silhouette accentuated by a cinched in belt.

She waved Sara over with a friendly smile.

"Hello pretty lady. I'm Jennifer, what can I do for you

today?"

"I'm here to see Mitch. I'm Sara Morrison from *High Gloss* and I'm interviewing him for an article we're running."

"It's nice to meet you, I'm the one who set up the interview with your assistant. I'm Mitch's business partner," she replied.

"Oh. I didn't know he had a business partner."

"It's only a new arrangement. I'm the brains behind the operation," she winked. "Now you, you look like you've got virgin skin," Jennifer purred.

"I do, and it's going to stay that way for a little bit longer," laughed Sara. "I am going to get a tattoo, but not today - that's for some follow-up blog posts."

"Well that's too bad. The boys here would love to get their hands on that creamy skin of yours. Mmmm..." Jennifer mused, running a lacquered nail down a schedule on the laptop. "Mitch is just finishing up with a client now, and I thought I'd slotted you in afterwards... but he's got himself clocking out for the afternoon."

She looked up and grinned at Sara, "but seeing as I'm good at bossing the boss, I'll make it happen."

As she spoke, the door to one of what appeared to be several private tattoo rooms opened and two men came out, laughing and chatting.

"Thanks man. Seriously, this looks amazing – way better than I imagined. I'm stoked."

"Happy to have had the opportunity to work on you. I haven't done Japanese art in a while, I might have to get myself another dragon – it's a timeless piece."

They did the manly back slap thing and the client left, leaving Mitch to amble towards Jennifer, his eyes lazily travelling up and down Sara's body as his lips turned up in a smirk.

He is totally eye fucking me right now.

Sara's throat went dry and her mind blanked. Which made no sense, because she *always* dressed to impress and was immune to men checking her out. But this man? He had her panties damp.

He was tall and broad, wearing a plain white t-shirt that hugged a muscular chest and tattooed arms. Scruffy, dark blonde hair was offset by designer stubble on chiseled cheekbones, a strong jaw and full, sensuous lips. Lips that quirked up as he registered she was also checking him out.

Photos on the Internet *did not* come close to preparing Sara for the sheer masculinity of this man. For her reaction to him. She was shaken by the frission of desire that fizzed through her just by *looking* at him.

On her quest for The One she'd been on a relentless schedule of dating that meant she'd been on dates with half of Sydney's male population. Before Phil, none made it past the third date. So yeah, she was a seasoned pro at meeting men. But she'd never known herself to have a physical reaction like this.

What was she, a schoolgirl?

Shaking herself mentally she took a determined step forward with an outstretched hand.

"Hi, I'm Sara Morrison from *High Gloss*."

"And what can I do for you, Sara Morrison from *High Gloss*?" he drawled without a hint of recognition, stepping so close that Sara was inches from his rock-hard body. She could practically feel the heat radiating off him.

Being in such close proximity meant Sara had to look

up, way up, to see his face and her traitorous legs went a bit shaky. Dear god he was perfection.

Until he opened his mouth.

"I think I'm going to marry you."

———

What the fuck had he just said?

He should try and take it back, but he was unable to move. He breathed in deep. Damn she smelled good - warm tones of wood and amber. He wanted to lick her neck. Hell, he wanted to lick her everywhere.

She was not his usual type. He liked chicks with an edge; bold and brash rockabilly girls, or the model-types that were there for a good time, not a long time. This one? Yeah. She clearly came from money. She was polished and confident, perfect makeup and not a single hair out of place. An ice princess. And *fuck* he wanted to make her melt and muss up all that perfect hair.

Seeing the faint red glow on her cheeks, he bent down, whispering just an inch from her pretty, shell-like ear, "I bet I could make you blush all over, Princess."

"Are you serious?" she spat, shaking back sleek, ashy blonde hair. "I'm here to interview you, you jerk."

"Interview me?" he ran a hand absentmindedly through his already disheveled hair. Oh yeah, he did remember that. He'd cancelled it on his schedule but forgotten to tell Jennifer about it. She was going to be pissed.

Media coverage about the business was fine, but he wasn't keen on a feature article that was about him. He didn't hide his impoverished childhood, but he sure as hell didn't mention it, either. And there was a little too much dirt in his past for a journalist to be digging around in, thanks anyway.

"We scheduled on Monday, but I'm guessing you've forgotten."

She was cute when she was pissed. Who knew ruffling the feathers of this little princess could be such a turn on?

Get her huffy and she crosses her arms and they push up those amazing tits… interesting.

Whatever. He wasn't doing the interview and she wasn't his type. Not going there.

"Yeah, about that. I'm going to have to cancel. Personal interviews aren't really *my* thing," he gave her a faux apologetic look.

"Well, being unprofessional isn't really my thing. You committed to this interview and we've already reserved pages in the next issue and booked advertising based on the article," she narrowed her eyes at him, long inky lashes sweeping against high cheekbones.

Were her eyes violet? They were hot as fuck, but couldn't be real.

"So how about you get your shit together and reschedule an interview for when it's *convenient* for you," she suggested, those violet eyes staring directly into his.

His cock twitched at her feisty attitude. That perfect creamy skin of hers was flushed and damn if he didn't want to see if he could get her to flush all over. He took a deliberate step forward to crowd her personal space, daring her to back down. She didn't.

He'd bet money that getting inappropriate would be enough for her to walk away. He was doing her a favour, what did it matter that he was going to have fun doing it?

"Is that what you really want, Princess? Want to spend some time with me, get up close and personal? I seem to remember something about inking you as part of the deal, and I've got to tell you, I can't wait to get under that skin of yours."

Her breathing hitched and he could swear her pupils were dilated in lust. Making women feel this way wasn't new to him, but liking the effect so much was a novelty – maybe LA hadn't jaded him as much as he'd thought.

"You're doing the interview, Mitch," Jennifer said grimly from the reception desk. She'd just hung up the phone and tuned into the conversation.

Ah fuck.

"I have plans right now," he shot back at Jennifer.

Glaring, she turned to address Sara. "Sorry to have inconvenienced you, Mitch can be a dick sometimes," she said sweetly. "He's definitely doing the interview. Any chance you could fit him in tomorrow?"

He saw the ice princess hesitate. He knew he'd pissed her off, but she still wanted the interview.

"He can come to you," Jennifer rushed on. "Whatever's easiest."

Nodding her agreement, Sara startled when the door opened and a leggy brunette waltzed in.

"Oh god, the traffic is a *nightmare* at the moment! So sorry I kept you waiting," she cried, ignoring Sara and Jennifer and draping herself over Mitch. "I can't wait to pick up where we left off last night," she said suggestively, pulling his head down to lock lips.

It was a sexy, open-mouthed kiss, and completely

inappropriate for the present situation. Compounding the awkwardness, for the life of him he couldn't remember her name. To be honest, what he'd really been looking forward to this afternoon was hitting the beach.

Since when would I rather surf than tap a fine ass like this?

Since Sara stood glaring at him, those violet eyes flashing. Damn, if looks could kill, he'd be a bloody mess on the floor. He disentangled himself from Mandy. Or was it Miley? Michelle?

He was really setting the asshole bar high today.

"Just give me a second, okay?" he set Mandy/Miley/Michelle aside and tried to get Sara to meet his gaze. Yeah, she was pissed.

"So, tomorrow?"

"Fine. I'll have my assistant email the details."

And she was gone, swishing that rich-girl hair and sashaying those long, long legs. Legs that he'd like to have wrapped around his waist right about now.

"Did you have to be such an assshole?" reprimanded Jennifer, looking up from the computer and giving him a narrow look. "This is going to be good for business Mitch. I need you on your best behavior."

"Yes ma'am."

CHAPTER 2

Sara was still fuming about what an arrogant jerk Mitch Smith was the next morning. Her morning walk along the coastline between Bondi and Bronte had failed to calm her, and usually salty air and exercise could fix anything.

Apparently not this.

Kicking off her sneakers at the door of the apartment, she dropped her groceries onto the kitchen counter.

She preferred not to think about *why* the man had her so riled, as a rule she normally didn't let guys close enough to affect her emotions. Not that it was ever an issue, because you couldn't really get close to someone over the course of three dates. And Phil certainly didn't raise her blood pressure.

Intense dislike on a first meeting was rare, however. How could one man piss her off so thoroughly in, like, 10 minutes?

She just had to keep occupied, to stop herself thinking about him. And stop thinking about the fact that he was sexy as hell. Right before he'd opened his mouth she'd been ready to jump his bones. Literally. He exuded some kind of raw, masculine sexuality that had short-circuited her normally reserved brain. Which was insane, because along with a three-date strategy, she also had a Closed Legs Policy, which even Phil hadn't breached yet.

Just because she'd dated prolifically didn't mean she put out. Like, ever. So maybe that was it, she reasoned. Her sexually deprived body had finally rebelled against the self-imposed restrictions.

Her phone rang as she opened a new punnet of strawberries and popped one in her mouth.

"Sophie!" she exclaimed, trying not to choke in her excitement.

"You didn't have to answer on the first ring, you could have swallowed first," her best friend, Sophie, laughed.

"Oh Soph, I miss you! Tell me you're coming back to Sydney soon to visit. I can't believe you're getting hitched to a farmer who lives in the middle of nowhere. It's *highly* inconvenient for me."

"So you tell me every time we talk. I'm so sorry that meeting the love of my life and having his baby is so disastrous for you," Sophie joked.

"Yeah yeah, you sound real sorry. Let's not rub salt in my single girl wounds. I'm actually glad you called, I needed someone to bitch to."

"Ooo, are things over with Phil already?"

Sophie was well versed in Sara's dating habits.

"No, it's not Phil. He's a whole other conversation. It's this guy I'm meant to interview for the magazine, I met up with him yesterday and he's a total jerk. It's just shitty that my first opportunity to write a proper, in-depth article has to be with some self-made tattoo artist. He's arrogant and self-assured and too hot for his own good."

"Too hot for his own good? Since when do you get hot and bothered by a man? You've always got the upper hand, leaving the poor guy to dangle at the end of your leash. I bet you've already got the Dear John letter to Phil in your email drafts."

"I'll have you know I dump over the phone, not by email.

That's so tacky."

Her laugh was a little too high – Sophie was uncomfortably close to the truth. Sara was aware that her insecurities often manifested as shallow behavior, and it was definitely not one of her finer personality traits. Neither was the annoying but ingrained desire to please her parents...

It was just that the dating scene was *brutal*, and she was secretly beginning to despair of ever achieving romantic happiness. Finding a relationship that would match her parents expectations was seeming less and less realistic.

Even so, it was good to talk with Sophie. Sara had been missing her ever since she'd been whisked out west and fallen head over heels in love, although she was happy for her friend and, having met her fiancé – Robert – she totally understood the willingness to move to the ends of the earth for him. He was delicious.

But that didn't mean she didn't miss her like crazy. They chatted for another 10 minutes and hung up after Sara had promised to put together a page on pregnancy beauty products so she could send the freebies to Sophie. Being a beauty editor definitely had its perks.

With that thought in mind, Sara pulled out the jar of coconut oil that she'd also picked up at Harris Farm. She was writing a column on the ways coconut oil could be incorporated into your beauty regime, and it was time for some hands-on research. First up was oil pulling for oral hygiene – it was the Ayurvedic practice of swishing oil around your mouth and was supposed to cleanse your teeth and gums of bacteria.

Sara again questioned her dedication to her job as she spooned a mouthful of the solid coconut oil, forcing herself not to gag as she let it melt in her mouth. Once it was liquid, she busied herself putting away the groceries as she swished it around, finding it a strangely enjoyable experience. Until someone knocked on her door.

She hesitated, not expecting Mitch for another half hour. When the knock sounded again, she shrugged and headed for the door. She opened it and almost choked, shutting it again quickly. With her back to the closed door she softly banged her head against it.

No fucking way.

The knock this time was followed by an amused snicker.

"That wasn't very polite Sara Morrison from *High Gloss*."

Closing her eyes she counted to five. Then ten. She knew he was still there. She could *feel* his presence.

"I'm not going anywhere Princess."

Gritting her teeth she reluctantly re-opened the door. Keeping her lips firmly closed, her eyes unwillingly drank in the sight of Mitch Smith lounging against her doorframe. The man had a *dimple* in his cheek for fuck's sake. That was totally stacking the odds unfairly in his favour.

"Not going to say hi?" he drawled, raising an eyebrow.

She huffed through her nose and, rolling her eyes, backed away from the door and headed to the kitchen sink so she could spit. Her skin prickled, alerting her to the fact he had followed.

"Should I even ask?" he laughed.

If Sara had been at a height disadvantage with Mitch yesterday when she was wearing heels, right now with her bare feet she felt ridiculously small. Drawing herself up as tall as she could, she snapped her eyes to him.

"What the hell are you doing here?"

"Uh, we have an interview?"

"You're early."

"Yesterday you were accusing me of being unprofessional. I thought I'd make amends. That, and Jennifer has threatened me bodily harm if I don't co-operate," he added sheepishly.

"I was going to meet you out the front."

"Your assistant. Becky, is it? She gave me your apartment number, so I came up. You should probably talk to her about giving out your home address to strange men on the phone. Bit of a security risk, that."

"You think?" Sara's sarcasm was biting.

"Well, I'm here now," he said with a conciliatory shrug of his massive shoulder. Sara was momentarily distracted by the way his snug t-shirt showcased flexing muscles with just that slight movement.

"And I read one of your columns, it was good."

"You bought a copy of *High Gloss*?" she asked incredulously, shaking her head. "No way. You wouldn't have been caught dead with a women's fashion magazine in your hand. It'd ruin your street cred."

"My street cred it just fine. I'd have no problem buying your magazine *and* a box of tampons." That smirk was infuriating. "But I looked it up online. I like the glasses you're wearing in your profile photo – nice touch."

Sara groaned inwardly. She'd been meaning to change that pseudo intellectual photo.

He was watching her with those blue eyes of his, a small smile playing around the corners of his sinfully delicious mouth.

Must stop thinking about how beautiful his lips are.

"The column was about organic honey wax and trends for shaping pubic hair," he continued.

Instantly her cheeks flushed and she fought to regain some semblance of control over the situation.

"How did you find the time to stalk my writing? I assumed you were otherwise engaged when I left yesterday," she managed to say, despite her fluster.

Curiously, she realised she didn't have an issue with having him in her home. Apparently as long as a serial killer was associated with her work and gorgeous, she was fine with being murdered. Who knew?

"She was a distraction I thought I needed. But then I saw something I wanted more."

He stepped further into the kitchen and instinctively Sara backed up. She wasn't afraid of Mitch, she was afraid of herself. Afraid she might throw herself into those strong, inked arms of his. Lust had spiked her blood and she'd be surprised if he couldn't hear her heart hammering in her chest.

What the hell is happening to me?

"You better not be referring to me buddy, because I don't date men like you."

"Oh Princess, I don't want to date you," his voice was a low, throaty growl. "I want to fuck you."

———

Mitch had made his excuses to the model about two minutes after Sara had left yesterday. He'd had a raging hard on, but it wasn't for the woman who was suggesting she blow him in the back room of his studio.

And while he'd never had a problem with fucking one

woman while thinking of another (hell, the other was usually in the bed too), the only lips he wanted wrapped around his cock were the lush ones that were currently parted in disbelief.

"You're crazy. Delusional. You need to leave." Sara actually stamped her barefoot on the ground.

Looking at her in those super tight exercise leggings made his balls tighten. And she'd crossed her arms under her chest again – putting that gorgeous cleavage on display. Getting her huffy definitely had its advantages.

But he had arrived unannounced and entered without an invitation. He was absolutely pushing the boundaries.

"So the interview is cancelled?" he asked, taking a step backwards towards the front door.

He didn't give a damn about the interview, in fact his coming on strong was all about dissuading her. But all of a sudden he had a new purpose – getting into Sara's panties and working her out of his system. He had no idea why this little firecracker was having an effect on him, but he was positive one good fuck would fix the problem.

The thing of it was, something about her blew all rational thought and primal instinct kicked in. And that instinct was telling him he needed her legs wrapped around his waist.

Now.

He tried to take a deep breath to control what was happening. All that did was draw her tantalizingly fresh scent into his nostrils, which flared in appreciation. Her breath was sweet and scented by coconut, and whatever fragrance she was wearing was light and fresh, with notes of apple and pear. What was she, a goddamn fruit salad?

And hell if he didn't want to eat some of that.

"You smell different."

"What?" she raised her eyebrows incredulously and shook her head.

"Yesterday, it was a woody, amber scent, and today you're all fresh and fruity. What's with that?"

"Are we seriously talking about my perfume?"

Forgetting himself, he took a predatory step forward and, not touching her, lowered his head to breathe deeply at her neck. She was warm and sweet and he'd put money on the fact she was aroused. She shivered, and that creamy skin flushed a little. Yep, she might not want to, but she wanted him.

"What can I say? It turns me on when a woman smells good," he murmured, pulling back slightly so he could look down at her upturned face. Her eyelashes had fluttered closed and she'd sucked a corner of her bottom lip into her mouth. The fact she wasn't trying to be erotic, made it more so. What he wouldn't give to suck on that lip.

He raised one finger and ran the big calloused pad of it down the side of her cheek. Her eyes sprang open, bringing them both back into the here and now.

"Look, I need this interview. But not here. I was planning on walking with you to a café on the corner," she said.

He weighed up his options. There was a high chance Jennifer would maim him if he didn't go through with this. And while the only time he wanted to spend with Sara was between the sheets, to taste her the once so he could move on, he admitted to himself that by introducing a physical element to their relationship he may be able to distract her from questions he didn't want to answer.

He wasn't accustomed to delayed gratification, but he also suspected Sara wasn't the kind of girl who was going to put out on the first date, no matter how hot he knew he was getting her.

"Okay, let's get a coffee."

He chuckled inwardly at the obvious relief on her face. The little princess didn't like him getting under her skin, and needed some space. He could give her space. But make no mistake, he'd have her begging for him to be inside her, real soon.

Out in the fresh air the sexual tension ratcheted down a notch, and he was surprised at how amiable their walk to get coffee was. As long as he could restrain himself from looking down at her snug fitting singlet, and not get close enough to smell her, he should be able to handle this. *Should* being the operative word.

"Do you live around here?" she asked, stretching her legs a little to match his long-legged stride, which he immediately shortened.

"Yeah, I bought one of the apartments above PACIFIC."

"Are you kidding? They're meant to be *amazing*!"

"I know, it was a little extravagant, but I figured it would be a good investment. I'll probably move to a more low-key suburb, like Bronte, when the studio is fully up and running and I'm not spending so much time there."

"I grew up in Woollahra, but moved to Bondi when I started college," she said. "I love the vibe here and I don't mind the tourists. I know it can get manic, especially during summer, but I love that they love my home as much as I do."

It figured that she grew up in Woollahra. He'd grown up on the streets of Western Sydney and if he hadn't made a name for himself in the inking world, there was not a chance his path would ever have crossed with hers.

He wondered what she'd think of him once she knew where he was from. Probably not much different from right now. Whatever her attraction to him – and that was undeniable – she sure as hell didn't like him. Probably knew she was slumming it, before he even told her where he came from.

They sat at a small table and chairs out the front of a café, and he stretched his legs out, letting them settle beneath her chair. Being tall had distinct disadvantages when he was in a restricted space like this, but right now he didn't mind the need to invade her personal space.

She looked at him without comment, and then primly moved her legs to the side to allow him room.

"So…" she took a deep breath. "To start with I just need to run over the details of the article with you – what we're going to cover and what the angle is, and then we can schedule a time to make it happen. The art director, Paul, will be in touch with you to organize the photo shoot, and then we need to talk about the process of, uh, my getting a tattoo."

"My favourite part of this whole deal," he drawled. "Where are we putting this tattoo?" He couldn't help a quick perusal up and down her luscious body. He was going to enjoy this, very much.

"I don't know, I was kind of hoping you might have some ideas…"

"Oh I have some ideas all right."

She blushed, and he found he was quietly amused. When was the last time he'd made a woman blush? The women he normally surrounded himself with weren't the blushing kind.

"I thought the first blog post could be about my initial

consultation with you, and then I'd follow that with a post about the options and the process, and then the actual tattooing." She visibly gulped at that, and he realized for the first time she was nervous about the tattoo.

"Do you want a tattoo?" he asked curiously.

"I think it'll make a good story. And they're going to syndicate the blog posts, so hopefully my byline will get more recognition."

"That's not what I asked Princess. Do you *want* permanent ink on your body?"

"I think so?" It was a question and not a statement.

"What were you thinking of getting tattooed?"

Her eyes strayed from his, and he could see she was uncomfortable. Easily he reached a long arm across the breadth of the table and held her chin with his thumb and finger, gently forcing her to face him. Blue eyes blinked at him. They were a shining blue today. The little minx changed the coloured contacts in her eyes as often as she changed her perfume. He wondered what her real eye colour was.

"Tattoos are a way of expressing yourself," he said softly, maintaining his hold on her face. "They don't just decorate your body, they record the stories of your life; there's a depth to them beyond the physical lines on the skin."

Releasing her, he sat back in his chair but kept his voice just as soft, loving that she unconsciously leaned towards him when he continued.

"The ink needs to mean something to you."

They stared at each other silently, undistracted by chatty patrons beside them, swooping seagulls or the passing foot traffic.

"I'm not going to ink you, Princess, unless you're truly

invested in it. Let's not waste my time, or yours."

She fiddled with the teaspoon next to her coffee and then glanced back up at him.

"Agreed. I'll make it worth your time."

Oh I'm sure you will princess.

CHAPTER 3

"So Sara, you've met with our tattoo artist. Where are you up to with the interview?" Bridgette, editor of *High Gloss*, looked over the top of her glasses and tapped her pen with customary impatience. She was a fair and thorough boss who valued time as the resource it was, and everyone at the conference table knew it.

Even though she had her notes meticulously in order, Sara scrambled slightly to answer. Bridgette did not look kindly on those who were unprepared in an editorial meeting.

"It's all set for this Friday and I'll have a first draft ready by Monday's editorial meeting."

Bridgette gave a nod of her head and looked back down at her notes, satisfied.

"So you've met him?" questioned deputy editor Pauline with a cheeky grin. "Is he as delicious as those photos we found online?"

Lily, the fashion editor, gave her a nudge with her elbow and raised her eyebrow. Pauline and Lily had been hanging over the back of Sara's desk chair when she'd initially researched Mitch, and the three of them had spent a good half hour Google stalking him.

"Girls! Not the time or the place," Bridgette rebuked. "Right, is there anything else we need to go over? I'm submitting the final pagination to the art department this afternoon."

When there was no comment from the conference table Bridgette rose perfunctorily and flicked a hand in farewell before exiting.

"God, it's like we annoy her and she would rather not interact with us at all," groused Lily, gathering her own scattered papers. "Never mind we're the ones who put together all the content for her precious magazine."

"I think she's under a lot of pressure from the big boss," said Sara, recalling a conversation she'd overheard in the lunchroom between head of accounts and one of the advertising girls. "Ad revenue isn't as high as it should be for this time of the year. No doubt she's getting ridden pretty hard about that."

"Trust me, no one is riding that woman!" giggled Lily.

"Forget Bridgette. Sara, we want details on spunky tattoo guy," interrupted Pauline. Standing, she rubbed her lower back and then attempted to balance her notebook on her eight-month pregnant belly. "I'm the size of a whale and ridiculously horny. Justin has never had this much sex before – he thinks he's going to keep getting me knocked up just so he can enjoy the perks."

They laughed together quietly, watching as the rest of the team left the room until it was just the three of them.

"So? Quit stalling. What was he like?"

Sara fidgeted with her fishtail braid, which was hanging over her shoulder. She looked between Pauline and Lily, who were her closest friends at work, and struggled to keep a blush from spreading over her face.

"Oh my god! You're blushing!" accused Lily. "You little tramp. Did you get it on with Hot Tattoo Guy?"

"Just do the interview before you date him. It'll totally get awkward to finish working with him after you dump him," said Pauline. "What? Don't look at me like that. You can't tell me you're serious about Phil."

"I kind of am serious about Phil. And I'm not dating Mitch! I'm *interviewing* him, for *work*. And besides, it doesn't matter how good-looking he is, he's a total douche. And can you imagine the reaction my parents would have if I dated the guy? Mum would need more than smelling salts to get over that."

Pauline and Lily looked at her expectantly.

"There's nothing to tell," Sara shrugged her shoulders in what she hoped was a dismissive manner. "He's not my type."

"Honey, with a body like that, he's *everyone's* type."

"Not mine."

"Oh that's right, because you only date suits who bore the pants off you, and then you dump them because there was no connection. Like Phil."

"Well, I'm still working on the connection with Phil, to be honest. But there's potential. His mother has already showed me the heirloom engagement ring his wife will wear."

"Seriously? That's kind of full on, Sar. Pauline's right," said Lily gently. "What if you don't have a connection with Phil because he's not your type? Maybe you need to reassess what it is you're really looking for."

What Sara was looking for was her very own Happily Ever After. And yeah, so maybe she was looking in a very narrow, parental-approved field. But surely within those parameters she could find a spark. She didn't believe in fairytales, but she did believe in chemistry – and, regardless of expectations, she didn't want to settle for a man who couldn't make her heart race.

There was no denying Mitch made her heart race. Hell, the man near gave her a heart attack when he got close – her pheromones definitely approved of his. But he wasn't the kind of man she could bring home to her parents; besides, he was a playboy who probably thought monogamy was a profane word.

She smiled fondly at her friends and headed for the door. "In the words of our fearless leader, now isn't the time or the place. Besides, I have to get to a product launch for some new self-tanning product."

"Oh the glamorous life of a beauty editor!" sang out Pauline. "Don't have too many glasses of champagne, you still have to come back to your desk this afternoon!"

Sara only had the one glass of champagne at the PR event and, after picking up the press kit had skipped out early, claiming deadlines. When she arrived back at her desk she found a gift bag with a large bow perched on top.

A normal girl would squeal with excitement, but for Sara it wasn't unexpected. As a beauty editor she had free products sent to her several times a week. She was on a first-name basis with most of the couriers who serviced the city.

Slipping off her three-inch Chloé lambskin heels under the desk she curled one leg under her and reached for the package. As inundated as she was with products, she appreciated when the PR girls got creative; this was a new shade of nail polish called Mexican Salsa and the PR company had paired it with a tiny cactus in a pot. Cute.

She was painting her nails coral red when one of the

advertising girls stuck her head around the door.

"Oh good, you've got the nail polish. I just got off the phone with their media agency and they've booked a double-page ad. You're going to need to include that product in the next issue."

Sara sighed and waved her off. She hated the commercial side of the publishing world, but felt slightly mollified that she did actually like this polish, so she wasn't totally selling her soul.

She did need to stop procrastinating though. Using deadlines as an excuse to leave the event early wasn't total BS – if she'd promised Bridgette a first draft of her article on Mitch by next Monday, and the interview was Friday afternoon, then she needed to get her background information organized.

She'd already researched Mitch's impressive career trajectory over in the US, where he'd worked under the Godfather of black and grey, Richard Grant – a legend on the ink scene who started in the underground punk world of the 70s and was extensively sought after.

Following in those footsteps, Mitch had become a favourite on the LA scene, and as well as inking the A-List set, he'd partied hard with them too.

But Sara wanted to go beyond what was already known, she wanted to know *how* he became the sensation he was today. Where did he come from and what was his driving force?

Because sure as hell that man had something driving him, and it couldn't be all testosterone.

Finding out what that was, however, proved elusive online until Sara stumbled across a link to a school reunion forum, which listed Mitch as a past student. Unsure if it was the same Mitch Smith she clicked on the class photos and immediately recognized his strong features. As a teenager he lacked the sheer bulk he now carried, but the promise of that body's potential was blatant.

She would bet the contents of her beauty bag that he'd set a record for breaking schoolgirl hearts – and she revered that damn beauty bag.

While south west Sydney was now a mecca of fine dining packed with renowned Vietnamese restaurants, back in the 80s and early 90s it dominated news headlines for its gang crime and a reputation as the heroin capital of Australia, and that was where 32-year old Mitch had been forged. What kind of upbringing had he had?

Sara was snapped back to the present with the ringing of her phone. Seeing it was her mother she gave a soft groan and debated whether to answer the call. Her parents cherished her with a suffocating love that left Sara feeling stifled. As an only child the pressure her family placed on her to become what *they* wanted was enormous.

"Hello mother."

"Sara darling! I'm just about to pop in for a spa treatment, but I wanted to let you know that I've got a dress on hold for you at Carla Zampatti in Double Bay. It's a gorgeous black crepe sheath with a lace insert back, perfect for the Save The Children charity dinner."

"Mum, I can dress myself. And I haven't even agreed to go to that dinner yet."

"Oh darling, you know I know what looks good on you. And of course you're coming to the charity dinner, your father and I expect it. Besides, it would be an excellent opportunity to cement things with Phil. Darla was only just saying it could be a good idea to make a reservation at the yacht club for the engagement party, you know how far out in advance they're booked."

Sara took a deep breath, trying to ignore the sinking feeling in her stomach. Darla, Phil's mother, would not make for an easy mother-in-law.

"Mum, Phil and I have only been a couple of dates. Let's not start planning the nuptials just yet, okay?"

"Oh darling, stop being so sensitive. You know I'm just excited for you."

Sara sighed.

"I'll try the dress on mum, but no promises."

———

"You're in a foul mood, mate. What's up?"

Having just finished a heavy-duty weights session with his friend Simon, Mitch was hoping he'd feel looser. More relaxed.

But he was still wound tight as a nun's habit.

Rolling his shoulders he wiped sweat from his forehead and glared at Simon.

"Nothing," he grunted. "Ah shit, sorry mate. Didn't mean to take it out on you."

"You didn't take it out on me, you took it out on yourself on the bench press. And your triceps are going to be letting you know about it tomorrow."

Simon was right. And there was a short answer to his current mood – Sara. He was irritated Jennifer was forcing him to do an interview that could unearth more than he was comfortable with. The fact that he couldn't get her out of his head was *beyond* irritating.

The two of them headed out of the gym towards the lift, which would take them up to Mitch's penthouse-style apartment. As they entered the apartment Simon let out a low whistle of appreciation, "I know I've said it before, but this is a *sweet* digs. You've sure come up in the world from when we started our apprenticeships together."

"You should've come to LA with me, you wouldn't believe the cash that gets thrown around over there. Blew my mind. Happy to be back here though, and to be working with you again."

They'd been 17-year old high school dropouts who'd met at the Red Rose Tattoo Palour and, although they'd been equally talented when it came to drawing and inking, Mitch was the one who'd always had the drive.

He hadn't just taken an opportunity to work in the US, he'd *made* the opportunity. As soon as he'd returned to Australia he'd looked Simon up and promptly poached him from a rival studio. He was now working at Ink Inc. and was one of the business' best assets.

"Mitch!" an over-excited three-year old launched across the spacious interior to fling herself into Mitch's arms. He caught her easily, and tossed her into the air.

"Hello my Apple, how was daycare today?" His niece Ruby was the apple of his eye, literally. Hence the nickname.

It was because her worthless, piece of shit father had walked out on Mitch's sister, Maggie, that Mitch had made the decision to leave LA and come home. Maggie had needed him, so he'd come.

Simon was hanging back, watching this interaction with curiosity.

"Man, I know we didn't stay in touch while you were away, but did you forget to tell me you had a kid?"

Mitch huffed out a laugh and disentangled himself from Ruby, dropping her lightly to the floor and tugging her pigtails affectionately.

"Nah, as if any kid of mine would turn out this normal. This is Maggie's daughter, Ruby," as he said this he watched Simon closely through lowered lids.

He was well aware that back in the day Simon had harboured a not-so-secret crush on his little sister, and he knew that it was only respect for their friendship – and probably the fear of Mitch's fists – that had stopped Simon from pursuing anything.

Simon understood that Mitch took his family obligations seriously. After all, as teenagers they'd both been willing to risk jail time to protect Maggie.

That said, since they'd reconnected Simon had been careful to avoid mentioning Maggie, and as her and Ruby had only just moved in, it was understandable he was surprised by the fact she had a child.

Maggie walking over to them saved Simon from a response, although the sudden fumbling with his gym bag and his inability to meet anyone's eyes was an answer in itself. Funny, Mitch had always thought Simon was smooth with the ladies.

Apparently not.

"Simon, hey. It's nice to see you again," smiled Maggie as she pulled Ruby into a hug. Even though Maggie was petite, she'd always had a vivaciousness that had made her appear bigger. But since Roger, her ex, had left she'd seemed deflated and diminutive, and Mitch was worried about her. Which is why he'd insisted they move in with him until Maggie got back on her feet.

Roger had not only whored around, he'd also drained all their bank accounts and was delaying the legal process, leaving Maggie basically destitute. She was a proud woman, and not thrilled to be living with her brother. And it didn't help that his apartment was all kinds of over-the-top flashy, especially when you considered the childhood home they'd grown up in.

Simon was right when he'd said it was a sweet digs. The vaulted ceilings and extensive glass optimized the sense of space and light and although the colour palette was neutral, timber and marble finishes gave it warmth and texture. The private heated plunge pool on the outdoor terrace was a bonus.

"Mummy, where is my rainbow drawing? I want to show Uncle Mitch," demanded Ruby, pulling away from her mother and skipping to a backpack that was lying haphazardly on the floor. "And then can I watch The Wiggles?"

"Sure baby girl, but you need to put that backpack away first." Stepping closer to Mitch she lowered her voice, "And you had a visitor this afternoon, some Anna Kournikova look-alike whose breast implants were so unrealistic that Ruby asked me why her boobies looked like that. I know this is your place, but we've talked about you bringing women back here while Ruby and I are staying. It makes me uncomfortable."

That description wasn't ringing any bells for Mitch – hell, it could apply to half the women he associated with. And wasn't that saying something about his moral character? But he sure as hell hadn't invited anyone up – since he'd moved in the only woman who'd been here had been his sister. And even if she and Ruby hadn't been staying, he'd never been one for having women in his personal space – he much preferred the anonymity of hotel rooms, or going back to the woman's place. Easier to leave that way.

"Shit Maggie, sorry. I wasn't expecting anyone. Did she leave a message?"

"Just that she'd be at Ivy tonight, and was looking forward to seeing you. Which made me wonder if you were still good to look after Ruby? I'm pulling a double-shift."

Maggie was an ER nurse, and since Roger had skipped out she'd been picking up as many shifts as she could. It was killing Mitch to see her working her ass off and stressed about money, when he was more than willing, and able, to take care of her.

It was something he'd been doing from the day she was born, and he'd proven before he'd do anything for her. And he didn't regret a single thing. He'd do it all again, even if this time it landed his ass in jail. Which was just one more reason he needed to remember Sara was more than a pretty face. She was a journalist who had the power to make his world fall apart if she dug too deep.

Mitch suspected the only reason Maggie had agreed to move in with him in the first place was because she was putting Ruby before her own pride.

"I'm not planning on going anywhere tonight, we're all good. Although as soon as you leave we'll probably sneak out to pick up some gelato," he teased, heading for the fridge to grab a cold sports drink.

"Want one?" he called out to Simon, who was still standing in the doorway watching as Maggie got Ruby set up in front of the television.

"I'm going to get changed into my uniform, I've got to leave in five," Maggie called out.

Throwing a drink bottle at Simon's head, Mitch gave his friend a warning look. "Don't go having any inappropriate thoughts about my sister in a nurse's uniform. She wears scrubs, not the kind of nurse outfit you pick up on Oxford Street."

"Whatever," Simon mumbled, guzzling from the drink. Having drained it in one go, he threw the empty container back to Mitch, aiming for his head and putting some force behind it. "You still haven't told me what had you pounding the weights so hard. I thought that with your extracurricular activities you wouldn't have the strength for a workout like that," he smirked, "Although maybe that's why you need to work on your arms, so you can –"

"What's extracurricular mean?" Ruby had abandoned her television show and honed in on Simon. The kid made it a sport to make strangers fall in love with her in five seconds flat. She was adorable.

"Forget about Simon, he doesn't know what he's talking about Apple. Why don't you go and find your shoes, and we'll walk mummy downstairs and then go and get some gelato?"

As Ruby took off he purposefully asked Simon work-related questions to avoid having to return to their previous conversation. He was being a tetchy bastard because a certain ice princess had invaded his head and since meeting her he hadn't been with another woman, which was very definitely out of character. He just couldn't figure out why *her*.

Still mentally shaking his head at himself, the four of them headed downstairs and while Simon and Ruby stopped in the doorway to compare sizes on their matching converse sneakers he pulled Maggie onto the sidewalk.

"Mag, I know you're catching the bus to work, but promise me you'll get a cab home – you're going to be falling asleep on your feet."

"Yeah yeah big brother. I've got it covered."

"I'm serious Maggie. I really wish you wouldn't work so hard," he raised a hand and touched her cheek tenderly, smiling a crooked smile.

"It is what it is. But thanks for looking after Ruby; I don't know what we'd do without you. That kid adores you, you know that right?"

"She's only female, how could she resist?" he joked, putting his arm around her and tucking her against him. "Go on then, isn't that your bus?"

In the rush of Maggie saying goodbye to Ruby Mitch's eyes snagged on a woman seated in a bus that was pulling out. He could have sworn it was Sara… all that gorgeous ashy blonde hair hanging over her shoulder in a Viking-like braid. The bus departed and he shook his head. Jesus, he was seeing random blonde women on buses and fantasizing it was Sara. What was it about this woman that wouldn't get out of his head?

"Come on Apple, let's go and ruin your appetite for dinner."

CHAPTER 4

Perched in the barber salon's luxurious swivel chair, Sara looked at herself in the mirror and had to give kudos to the Lancôme concealer she'd applied liberally that morning – she still looked fresh and dewy, with no sign of the dark smudges beneath her eyes she'd awoken with.

She'd tossed and turned in bed last night, remembering the sight of Mitch Smith she'd accidentally witnessed from the bus.

She'd been on her way home and was still thinking about that school photo she'd found of him. She didn't want to be looking forward to seeing him again, but she couldn't deny that even if intellectually she wanted to slap his arrogant face, physically she wanted to… Jesus, she didn't even know what she wanted to do. She just needed to ease the ache between her legs and the full body flush that accompanied it. And by all accounts it was a reciprocated feeling; he'd already warned her he wanted to fuck her.

Maybe that was the allure. She'd never had a man speak to her that way before. She'd never had a man fuck her before.

She hadn't even been looking out the bus window, more just staring at the reflections in the glass, when he'd caught her eye. Standing there on the sidewalk with a small, pretty woman dressed in surgical scrubs. From everything she knew of this man, the woman was far from his usual type. And his face had appeared soft, not sexual, as he spoke to her. When he raised a hand to gently touch her cheek and then tucked her in against his side, Sara had a jolt of pure, unadulterated jealousy.

She actually felt her insides curl up and in response her breath caught as though she was in pain. No, not pain. Just a shudder of surprise that made her feel vaguely sick. She had absolutely no claim on this man, so her reaction was as shocking as it was unwarranted. The relief as the bus had pulled away was palpable.

But then she'd spent the night alternating between incredulity that he obviously had real feelings for a woman, crippling sadness that now she would never know what it was like to be with him, and then a scorching anger at herself for missing something she'd never even had, with a man who was most definitely *not* her type.

At work she'd been uncharacteristically snappy; it irritated her that this man was occupying so much of her brain space – his life and his relationships should not concern her and she couldn't understand why she was getting so affected. It was totally *not* cool.

The only thing that had got her through the day was knowing she'd see Marc this afternoon. He'd started cutting and colouring her hair back when he was an apprentice and she was a junior writer; he now owned a swanky barber shop, with a clientele of mainly men. Sara didn't care it was a barber and not a hair salon, she was loyal to Marc and loved it here.

As she thought that, the man in question swanned across and leant over her shoulder to peer at her in the mirror.

"Damn girl, those eyelashes are knockout. Who did them and where?" he demanded, before spinning her chair so she was facing him. He grabbed a rolling stool from behind and straddled it so they were facing each other. "I've been thinking about getting some falsies, but I'd want them longer than yours."

The man had the most divine chocolate brown eyes with lashes that were already ridiculously long. He did not need to enhance them. Marc was boyish-looking, attractive and slender; he dressed impeccably and his over-the-top camp mannerisms only scaled back when he was asleep. Barely.

Sara adored him.

"They're Russian Volume Lashes, I got them at Lady Lash who have just opened in Pitt Street. Pretty amazing, huh?" she fluttered them flirtatiously at him.

"And I'm vibing those navy eye contacts – totally hot. Who is on the date schedule at the moment? Finished with Phil yet?"

Sara's standing weekly appointment with Marc for a wash and blow dry meant he was intimately acquainted with her search for The One.

"Hang on, before you answer let me guess, you've had the third date and flicked his sad little ass, and now you're working your way through a list compiled by mummy and daddy. Hmmm?" he raised knowing eyebrows at her. "Baby girl, I'm thinking you need to shake things up a bit, look outside the square. You feeling me?"

Sara swatted affectionately at him and then turned her chair back around, maintaining eye contact through the mirror.

"You don't get any details from me until you bring me a coffee. Where are your manners today?"

His mouth stretched into a Cheshire Cat grin and he

flounced away to direct an apprentice, who walked over to them moments later with two champagne flutes.

"It's after five o'clock, we can totally justify a champagne," Marc purred. "And I wanted to show you these shots from the Dior catwalk, how fabulous are the lilac streaks in this model's hair – she's the same ashy blonde as you and I totally think you'd rock the look."

Glancing at the proffered iPad Sara nodded in agreement, "Totally hot, I love it. But can you imagine the look on my parent's face if I did something like this? They can't even handle when I go too heavy on the eyeliner."

"Hmmmm, those parents of yours…" Marc pursed his lips. "I'm not sure they're a good influence on you."

Sara just laughed at him and took a sip of the champagne, concentrating on the iPad even as she felt a client sit down to the left of her.

"So you've finished with Phil, am I right?"

"No, I haven't finished with Phil," she replied, a touch defensively. "We saw each other twice last week, although he had to work over the weekend, something about getting a deposition ready because a court date had been moved forward."

"Oh darling, he bores me silly and I've never even met the man. Where on earth do you come up with these suits?"

"Oh stop it, he's quite handsome you know. Excellent husband material."

Marc rolled his eyes.

"I'm seeing him tomorrow - we're going to Icebergs, I'm more excited about their gin and tonic cured ocean trout than I am about seeing him, to be honest," she admitted with uncharacteristic candor.

"So why keep seeing him? The ocean trout can't be that good."

Sara coloured a little and dropped her eyes, and Marc pounced. "Baby girl, why are you getting all coy on me? What haven't you told me?"

"It's not a big deal," she shrugged her shoulders. "We haven't kissed yet, and I want to do that just to make sure, you know, there really is no chemistry there."

"Oh you would know if there was chemistry, even without the kiss," assured Marc with a knowing look.

Draining her champagne Sara sighed, "I just want to free fall into romantic bliss, but it never happens. You know that movie, *Legends of the Fall*?"

"Honey, it's got a young Brad Pitt in it, of course I know the movie."

"Well remember that scene, when Samuel is going to war and Susannah is being comforted by Tristan and there's this *moment*, when he's breathing at her neck and they *almost* kiss and it's the hottest thing ever. I want *that*, I want that kind of tension and desire…"

God, she can't believe she'd just said that.

One glass of champagne and she was exposing her innermost thoughts.

"Princess, if it's tension and desire you want, I'm right here," drawled a throaty voice that instantly made the hairs on Sara's arms rise.

What the hell is Mitch Smith doing here?

Sara knew her mouth had fallen open and she was helpless to stop the rising flush that bloomed on her cheeks. Slowly turning her head, she clocked Mitch's bulk lounging in the chair to her left.

Oh fuck, kill me now.

———

The hairdresser who'd been talking with Sara was glancing between the two of them with comic speed; his eyes alight with the drama. If Mitch hadn't been so focused on Sara's reaction, he'd have been tempted to laugh.

As it was, he was too intrigued. The princess was pining for a knock-your-socks-off kiss. Hell, he could deliver that. Why she had to look for it, however, was a mystery.

He'd been across the street from the barbers when he saw her arrive, and even as he'd mentally berated himself for acting like a stalker, he followed her in. All of a sudden his hair desperately needed a trim.

He hadn't been surprised to find her sipping champagne, of course that would be her drink of choice. She probably ate off silver spoons too. But the fact she was seeing some douchebag and hadn't even kissed him? Definitely surprising.

And while she didn't seem too keen about the date, Mitch still felt a tug of something that was suspiciously close to territorial, knowing she was going to be seeing another guy. Which was bat shit crazy, because what did it matter to him if she was seeing other guys? True, he had a massive case of blue balls over the woman, but he didn't want to date her. Hell no.

"Well colour me surprised, aren't you just a scrumptious piece of man," cooed the dude behind Sara. "I'm Marc, and welcome to my little barber shop. Can I take it that you've met my girl Sara before?"

Sara looked close to bolting. A delicious pink flush had suffused the delicate skin of her cheeks and she was determinedly not meeting his eye. What was it about her that had him so interested? She was classically beautiful, with high cheekbones, a heart-shaped face and large, expressive eyes. But he could do beautiful every night of the week if he wanted. It was her feisty attitude that caught his attention, and that sharp intelligence and wit. And who was he kidding? He was dying to get his hands on that virgin creamy skin of hers. She was a tattoo artist's wet dream.

"We've met," he answered, winking at Marc before returning his attention to Sara, "Haven't we Princess?"

"Baby girl, you've been holding out on me," scolded Marc, pinching her lightly on the upper arm. "Here I was thinking your taste in men sucked, when you've been broadening your horizons on the sly."

"In his dreams," she replied, snapping her eyes between the two men. "Marc, I think it's time we headed over to the washbasins, yes?"

Mitch couldn't hide a grin as she marched off, those sassy hips of hers swinging. Damn she had an amazing figure. And that attitude of hers was a hell of a turn on.

He settled back in the barber's chair and was surprised by the smile reflected back at him in the mirror. He couldn't remember the last time he'd been interested in a woman like this. He couldn't wait to melt the ice princess.

"Dude, are we really hitting this restaurant just so you can stalk a chick?" Simon grumbled as they settled at a terrace table at Icebergs, overlooking the iconic ocean pool.

"I told you, the ocean trout is meant to be good."

"If you're happy to pony up for the bill, I'm more than happy to eat here, even if I do feel like a wanker. Classy places like this give me the heebie jeebies."

Mitch didn't bother to respond, just kept scanning the restaurant to see if Sara had arrived. If following her into the barber had made him feel like a stalker, this was flirting with a restraining order and, while he couldn't have stayed away if he tried, he also didn't want Sara to see him. This was purely for observational purposes. If she was going to be digging through his past, then he sure as hell wanted to know what kind of person she was.

A waiter was taking their drink order when he saw Sara and her date enter, and all of his attention was drawn to tracking her movement.

"Sir?"

Tearing his eyes away he turned back to his table, reminding himself to behave civilly. It wasn't the waiter's problem that he was about to lose it seeing some other guy with his hand on the small of Sara's back.

"I'm sorry, what did you say?"

"You asked for Jack Daniel's; would you prefer Old No.7, or the Single Barrel?"

"Single Barrel. And make it a double please."

"I'm sorry, legally we can't sell double shots of spirits."

Damn he missed the loose liquor regulation of the States.

"Make it two glasses."

As the waiter left Simon raised his eyebrows and grinned.

"You're whipped. Who is this woman? I want to meet her."

Mitch didn't know how to respond to that. He had no idea

why he was behaving like this, over a woman who definitely wasn't his type. Although clearly that was the appeal, wasn't it? That, and the fact she didn't want to want him. Yeah, he'd always liked a challenge.

"Don't look now, but she's sitting behind you and to the right."

"My right or your right?" Simon asked as he blatantly swung around in his chair.

"Fuck! We're trying to be inconspicuous. Turn your ass back around and stop gawking."

As their drinks were delivered to the table Mitch drained the amber liquid in one glass, keeping his eyes trained firmly on Simon; "I'm not fucking around Simon, don't screw this up for me."

"She's pretty."

"She's beautiful."

"Yeah, she's rich-girl beautiful. Kind of not really in your league though, right?"

Mitch knew his friend wasn't trying to bust his balls. He wasn't being an asshole, just stating a fact. And he was right.

"It's not like I want to marry her. She's writing an article on me, and I need to know that she's legit. If she's going to be digging into my background…" he didn't finish his sentence, too intent on watching as Sara laughed at something her date had said. He wanted to be the one sitting opposite her. So bad. He wanted her looking at him with expectation and anticipation.

He refocused on Simon. "So yeah, I want to fuck her. She needs a good lay, and I'd bet my left testicle he can't bring her to orgasm."

He took a slug of his second whiskey.

"Ah hell, I don't know. I'm not really thinking with this, hence the *Fatal Attraction* moves."

"Yeah okay, cool. Let's just steer clear of boiling bunnies."

"Agreed."

The gin and tonic cured ocean trout could have been sensational, but Mitch was too absorbed in watching Sara's date to notice. He was interested to see that while Phil may have been "excellent husband material" – as she'd told Marc – he was failing to engage or animate Sara. Even from this distance Mitch could tell he was struggling and, in doing so, overcompensating. He didn't seem to draw breath as he talked on, and on.

In direct contrast to Mitch's own dining companion who, having given up on conversation, had pulled out his iPhone and was actively perusing Tinder in a bid to set something up for later in the evening.

"Mate are we finishing up here soon?" Simon looked up as their dinner plates were cleared away.

"Yeah, we're done."

Mitch wasn't sure what he'd hoped to achieve by being here tonight, and he was regretting coming. He'd already known Sara wasn't into her date, and he didn't like seeing her grow quieter over the course of her meal. She clearly wasn't enjoying herself, and her date clearly didn't give a damn. Jerk.

When Sara excused herself to the ladies room, Mitch decided it was time to abort this ill-advised mission. Standing at the front of the restaurant paying the bill, he was nudged in the back by Simon, who gestured with his chin. Phil had left the table to take a phone call, and was standing with his back to them, his voice loud enough to be audible.

"… looks the goods but she's dead boring. At least it's keeping my mum off my back. I'm just about to text Miranda to see if she's up for something."

What. The. Fuck.

Did he just infer that Sara was an uptight bitch?

Mitch was pocketing his credit card as Phil finished his phone call, and then intentionally planted himself in the other man's path, his broad shoulders and thickly muscled chest blocking the way. It didn't matter how slick Phil's hair was, or how expensive his bespoke suit – he was a little shit that didn't deserve to spend time in Sara's company.

"Ah… can I help you?" Taking in Mitch's tattooed bulk, it was clear Phil thought himself above such interruptions.

Mitch took a step forward and Phil took one back, primarily, Mitch suspected, so he didn't have to look up as he spoke. Men like Phil didn't like to make concessions, but they also didn't like to have their masculinity questioned.

And there was nothing like coming up against a male built like to Mitch to make you question that.

"Yeah, you can help me," Mitch growled quietly, not wanting to make a scene. "Don't talk like that about women. Ever. Especially not the one you're with."

He was tempted to drop his shoulder as he moved past Phil, just to leave him with a bruise to remind him of the warning, but settled instead for a hard stare with narrowed eyes. Better to leave the bastard nervous than righteously indignant.

Fuck, someone needed to talk to Sara about her taste in men.

CHAPTER 5

Shifting in the back seat of the taxi, Sara attempted to reason with her mother over the phone as discreetly as possible.

"I realise you're thrilled that I've seen Phil a couple of times, but I just don't want you to get your hopes up," she said. "I'm not even sure how serious I am about him – definitely not enough for you and Darla to be planning an engagement party."

For fuck's sake.

"Darling, she said yourself that finding a husband was a priority," reminded her mother, "and Phil comes from such a lovely family."

Sara muffled a sigh. It was true that, on paper, Phil appeared the perfect match. But she craved intimacy and connection, and she was ready to face the fact that Phil wasn't going to be the one to deliver on that score, no matter how good his pedigree.

"I need to go mum, just please refrain from discussing wedding venues with Darla, okay?"

Slipping her phone into her handbag she tried to ignore the hard lump in her stomach. She wasn't accustomed to disappointing her parents.

Looking out the taxi window, she realized she was almost at Bondi. She'd been keyed up about interviewing Mitch all day, and it hadn't helped that Bridgette had called her into her office before lunch just to reinforce how much was riding on it – not just advertising dollars and readership stats, but Sara's career progression as well.

She rested her head back on the taxi's headrest and closed her eyes momentarily. This bizarre attraction she felt towards Mitch was *not* going to mess with her professionalism. She was going to nail this story, and it was going to launch her from beauty editor to deputy editor. Well, acting deputy editor until Pauline came back from maternity leave.

As the glint of ocean sparkling in the taxi's windscreen heralded their arrival in Bondi, Sara checked her eyeliner and did a quick spritz of Narcisco Rodriguez parfum. Paying the cab driver and stepping onto the sidewalk she resolved to pretend Mitch had never overheard that cringe-worthy conversation with Marc. There was no reason to be awkward. If anything, he should have the decency to be embarrassed for listening in on a conversation that was clearly personal.

Although something told her that decency wasn't something Mitch Smith specialized in.

"Hello pretty lady, it's nice to see you again," Jennifer smiled. "Are you here to get all the dirt on our boy wonder?" she raised a perfectly plucked eyebrow, and Sara made a mental note to slot in a blog post on eyebrow trends next week.

"We'll see," she murmured as she took a seat on a black leather chair in the waiting area. Ink Inc. was a hotbed of activity with a melting pot of ethnicities – the only uniformity appeared to be the cool factor, with each and every client exuding their own brand of cutting edge style, along with a plethora of skin ink.

Discreetly watching them, the idea of getting a tattoo began to feel slightly less scary. It was liberating to see how comfortable they were in their own skin and Sara had to admit the majority of the artwork was just that, art. Well, except perhaps for the tattoo of a zombie unicorn gracing a petite woman's forearm. That was just odd.

"Hello Princess. I wasn't sure if you'd show."

All plans of professionalism dissipated as that throaty voice curled over her. The smooth, low timbre of Mitch's voice evoked all kinds of lust-driven thoughts and Sara's body instinctually reacted. While her heart rate increased and her nipples tightened, her mind blanked as she fixated on how that voice would sound whispering to her under the cover of darkness.

Oh dear god.

Standing before her, Mitch could have been some ancient warrior with this immense height, thickly muscled body and arms of intricate ink work. A Norse Viking come to life in scruffy denim jeans and a flat cap.

Sara blinked up at him, momentarily forgetting herself. Her surroundings. Her ability to breathe. What was it about this man that called to her on such a basic, primitive level? She was all but ready to present herself to be clubbed over the head and dragged back to his cave.

His customary smirk was the trigger that dragged her back to conscious thought and Sara flushed, hating that he had correctly interpreted her silence. She *so* did not want to be yet another woman falling at his feet.

With a shake of her hair she stood, choosing to ignore her traitorous body, which was goddamn *quivering* with delight at the sudden proximity to Mitch's hard masculinity.

"Are we doing this?" she asked with an arched eyebrow, hoping against hope he wouldn't see through her feigned nonchalance.

"I don't know, are we?" he countered with an eyebrow raise of his own.

"The interview Mitch. The interview."

"And do you blush such a becoming shade of pink with all your interview subjects, Sara Morrison from *High Gloss*?"

The mental image of Mitch on the sidewalk with that woman in surgical scrubs was just the impetuous she needed to shake off Mitch's flirty tone. He was a womanizer, plain and simple. She wondered briefly if that woman he'd been with knew just how much of man-whore he was.

"Don't kid yourself, it's warm outside. There isn't a thing you could say or do that would make me blush. Now, are we going to do this interview, or not?"

Sara was happy that her voice was level and calm, she knew if she'd been snappy he'd have taken that as a sign he was getting to her. And he wasn't. Not even a bit.

Well, maybe a tiny bit.

That faux calmness was tested when he leant in, bridging the gap between their bodies. "I like a challenge," his breath whispered at her ear, and Sara's own breathing hitched. "And I can't wait to make you blush. All over."

He pulled back and grinned wolfishly down at her, flashing that dimple.

Swallowing, Sara looked away, focusing on anything but the man taunting her. She would *not* dwell on the many and varied ways he could make her blush.

"Oh for goodness sakes Mitch, stop teasing the poor girl," called out Jennifer. "And give her the interview before she changes her mind."

That predatory smile flashed at Jennifer, before Mitch led

Sara into one of the tattooing rooms, closing the door firmly behind them. It was a large workspace; clean and simple and dominated by a wall of vibrant street art – the edgy graffiti similar to that in the main studio.

"This is incredible," Sara said, stepping back to fully admire the artistry.

"Thanks, it's where I started – street art. Well, graffiti really."

"You did this?"

"Yeah, I contacted the local youth outreach program and employed some local street kids to come in and do the art in the main part of the studio, and it got me itching to get back to my roots. Each of my tattoo artists have their own room, which is where they display their work, but I figured there was enough of my work on the website and our social media, so yeah, I filled this wall with my graffiti."

Gone was the cocky smirk, replaced by an earnestness that had a hint of, vulnerability?

As they settled at a small table and Mitch poured them both a glass of mineral water Sara considered this new information. She was intrigued at his hint of a less than salubrious beginning, and his act of helping out local disadvantaged kids.

"Look, I'll be honest with you Sara, I've done a lot of interviews. A lot. But they've always been about the celebrities I've worked with, tattooing trends… No one has ever asked the background questions that I know you're going to want. So just take it a bit easy on me, okay?"

Well wasn't this a turn around?

———

Mitch wasn't trying some new tactic with Sara, he was genuinely uneasy about the exposure she represented. And now they were behind a closed door, just the two of them – pared back with no distractions.

Her eyes, a warm whiskey colour today, skipped to his and held, narrowing slightly. "You knew this was going to be an in-depth feature article, don't tell me you're pulling out now?"

Stretching his legs out, he jigged his knee up and down. Jesus, was it getting hot in here?

"I'm not pulling out, I'm just, you know, asking you to be kind."

"Kind? To you?" her tone was incredulous and she tilted her head slightly to the side. "Come on Mitch, when have you ever had to ask a woman to be kind to you? Don't they usually just gaze adoringly into those baby blues and worship you?"

"Usually," he agreed drily, rolling his shoulders in an attempt to release some tension. "But I'm still waiting for you to fall into line with that one. I guess blue eyes don't do it for you."

"I like blue eyes just fine. It's your arrogance I find issue with," she countered, softening the statement with a smile. "You are ridiculously self-assured, which is either endearing or aggravating, depending on –."

"Depending on?"

"I suspect it depends on whether the woman in question is about to sleep with you, or has just been dumped by you."

"Ah, so I'm still endearing to you then?"

She huffed out a reluctant laugh and bent to retrieve a pen and pad from her handbag, unwittingly giving him an excellent view down the top of her dress into a tantalizing hint of cleavage.

Cue more knee jigging from him.

"Can we start the interview now?" she asked, motioning for his attention as she began recording on her iPhone.

"Sure, but can I just ask one question first?"

She gave a little sigh and hit pause on the recording, pen poised expectantly.

"What colour are your eyes?"

The eyes in question widened perceptibly and her tongue peeked out to do a quick swipe of her bottom lip.

"Seriously? That's your question?"

"They were violet when I first met you, and then blue. Navy when I saw you at the barbershop, and today they remind me of my favourite single malt. I can't decide which colour I like best, actually."

She seemed a little stunned that he'd obviously memorized every little detail from each of their encounters, and he wondered if he'd given too much away. Sure, she knew he wanted to bang her. Ferociously. But she didn't know just how often she'd had a starring role in his fantasies over the last week. And on second thoughts, it was probably better she didn't.

"You know what? A little mystery is good," he declared, settling back into his chair. "Let's just leave it at that and get this interview started."

"Sure. It's well known that you're a high school drop out —"

"It sounds so flattering when you put it like that," he said drily.

"But what's the why? *Why* did you drop out of school and

start tattooing?"

Mitch's jaw ticked. He wondered what Sara would say if he actually told her the truth. That he failed to keep his mother clean and she'd over-dosed. That to keep he and Maggie out of the foster system he'd left school so he could earn enough money to keep them fed.

"School didn't interest me, but I was always good at art. I saw an apprenticeship at the Red Rose advertised, and it looked like fun," he said offhandedly.

"It looked like fun?" she raised a skeptical eyebrow. "That's what you're going to give me?"

"Life doesn't have to be about climbing the corporate ladder, watching the stock market and comparing trust funds, Princess. It can be fun. I love what I do, and what is it they say? If you love what you do, you'll never work a day in your life."

"Great, I'll just make this story one big cliché," she muttered.

He softened. He really did respect Sara's commitment and her determination to do well with this feature. And hell, he and Jennifer had a lot to gain with the exposure.

"You're right, I'm being a jerk," he admitted. "I have reservations about you turning this into a 'rags to riches' type story – I'm not interested in my past being examined."

"You could have just been upfront with me about that," she huffed, but he could tell she was softening as well. "I can respect boundaries."

Over the next hour Mitch relaxed as the interview fell into an easy rhythm; Sara's questions were clever, thoughtful and sometimes unexpected. He appreciated the complexity and layers she was adding to the conversation, getting him to articulate elements of his life and career that he'd usually gloss over.

"So along with the resurgence of bold pigments, you're also seeing a lot more requests for Japanese tattoos, how do you feel about them?"

"Usually neo-traditional Japanese designs are big and intricate, and all the elements interact with each other, so they can be a challenge. What I need to consider, as the artist, is how a tattoo looks both up close, and far away. You've got to think about the whole picture as you're designing."

"And what kind of work do you like doing the most?"

"It doesn't really matter if it's a minimalist treble clef behind a musician's ear, or a double exposure artwork in black and grey across a surfer's back; it's just an incredible privilege to be trusted to make such a permanent statement on someone. A tattoo is only as consequential as its frame of reference."

"So it's personal?"

He looked up from re-filling their water glasses, completely focusing on the woman sitting across from him, letting the silence stretch as he watched her until she gave a little squirm in her chair.

They'd both been so focused on the gentle give and take of the interview process that, unbelievably, he'd forgotten for more than two minutes how eminently fuckable he found her. With the pause in conversation, it was suddenly all he could do to keep his hands to himself when what he'd really like to do was grab that tiny waist of hers and drag her into his lap.

"You better believe it's personal Princess," he all but growled, deciding it was time for a break in the interview. "And while we're making it personal, how did your date go with Mr Excellent Husband Material?"

Sara jabbed her finger onto her iPhone to stop the recording and scowled at him. "I knew it was too much to hope you wouldn't bring that up," she snapped. "If you had any manners at all you'd be embarrassed you blatantly listened in to a discussion that had absolutely nothing to do with you."

"I'm not at all embarrassed I overheard you wishing for, what were your words? 'Tension and desire'?"

"Oh god!" she flung her hands over her face, refusing to look at him. "Must you? Let's not relive the moment, okay?"

Fuck she was adorable.

Coming out of his chair and around the small table that separated them, he dropped to his knees before her and softly tugged her hands down from her flushed face. Her subtle amber scent damn near floored him. Dragging in a deep breath he concentrated on that lovely face of hers, while his thumbs lightly stroked the pulse points of her wrists.

"I think your friend Marc is right, you need to take a break from dating suits. Starting with breaking things off with that dickhead Phil." As she opened her mouth to protest, he continued; "I'm not saying I'm excellent husband material – hell, I know I'm not – but I can guarantee I'm excellent fucking material. And you and I? We have the sort of mad chemistry that will give you enough tension and desire to last you for the rest of your life, no matter which boring suit you marry."

Stunned, she just gazed at him, her chest rising and falling to the rapidly beating pulse he could feel fluttering in her wrists. Because of his six-foot four-inch height his eyes were level with hers as he knelt before her, but he resisted the impulse to lean closer. Not until she admitted to the sizzling attraction between them. There was no way this was just a one-sided temptation.

"So, we just –" she paused, "fuck? And that's it?"

"Well I'd recommend we do it more than once, just to ensure you get the full experience. But yeah, no dating, no relationship, just a little physical distraction before you keep looking for Mr Right."

Her arousal was obvious, those delicious lips of hers were slightly parted and her pupils were dilated. Even fully clothed, this was possibly the most erotically charged moment of his life. He wanted her *that* bad.

"I can be your Mr Right Now," he promised, wondering when this had become more than a challenge for him. Now, it was a god damn necessity.

Bending forward he brushed his lips across hers, smiling to himself as she mewled like a kitten and opened for him. Delaying the inevitable, he nipped at her lush bottom lip before dragging it into his mouth and sucking. As her hands rose to frame his face, pulling him closer, he gave in and thrust his tongue inside her, groaning at the stunning intimacy. Dropping her wrists he pulled her flush against his straining body, one hand holding the nape of her neck as he angled his head to better taste that incredible mouth of hers. Damn she was sweet.

The kiss blazed from passionate to incendiary in seconds and, fearing he was about to lose control, Mitch pulled back. Dropping a light kiss on her nose, he rested his forehead against hers as they both attempted to tame their breathless panting.

"Okay," she whispered. "I want this."

CHAPTER 6

Holy crap did I just say that?

She blinked her eyes open to find Mitch's blue stare just centimeters from her own. They were breathing shared air they were so close.

A passionless image of Phil flicked across her brain and she finally admitted to herself that she wouldn't be returning his calls.

She was hyper aware of Mitch; the texture of his skin, the tactile sensation of his rough beard stubble… those full lips of his that had just completely captured her.

And she did. She did want this.

Her breasts were heavy with arousal and aching to feel his touch, her nipples tightly beaded and visible against the fabric of her dress. She'd never been so completely out of her depth, and wanted nothing more than to dive in further. She wanted to drown in this man.

And yet he was still, unmoving. Kneeling before her with his head bowed against hers, breathing in the air she had just expelled.

"Mitch?" she couldn't help the tremulous tone, just as she couldn't disguise the need laced through that one word.

"You've got to give me a minute Princess," he groaned. "Otherwise I'm going to ravage you right here and now."

She bit her bottom lip.

"And that would be a bad thing?"

If he didn't touch her *now* she was going to explode. Heat pooled between her legs and instinctively she clenched her thighs together.

Experimentally she ran her hands up the outsides of his arms, over the solid muscle and taut, smooth skin to settle on the enormous breadth of his shoulders. Dear god this man was big.

In a fluid move his large hands clamped around her waist and, leaning back on his heels, he dragged her from her chair to straddle his lap. As he slid those talented hands up the back of her thighs to settle on her ass, the floaty fabric of her dress rode with his movement and bunched around her hips. She was suddenly very aware that she was positioned directly over the hard length of his erection, and the fabric of her underwear was damp with arousal. The heat that slammed into her was mortification, rather than desire. What if he realized her panties were so wet? Surely it wasn't normal to react like this, so wantonly? Unease settled, cold, in her stomach.

Could she do this? What if he realized that she wasn't like his usual hookups and decided it wasn't worth the hassle?

Fuck I wish I knew what I was doing with this man.

She wriggled in discomfit, which only served to seat her more snuggly against him. A throaty growl vibrated from his throat as he leaned back on his powerful haunches and then, holding her ass firmly, stood up as though she weighed next to nothing.

He gave a wicked grin at her surprise and without thinking Sara's legs clamped around his waist and her arms clung to his thickly corded neck. Her caveman fantasy was fast becoming a reality as her fears dissolved.

Walking over to the far wall, Mitch eased her back onto a bench, pressing firmly between her spread legs as he claimed her lips in a deep, drugging kiss. Her mind spinning, Sara lost herself to the feel of their lips tasting, meshing. His tongue ran along the seam of her lips and she opened for him without hesitation. Eagerly she met him thrust for thrust as he delved deeper, took harder. Distantly she felt skillful fingers working the zip at the back of her dress and in seconds the straps were slipping down her arms, the top of her dress pooling at her waist. Hell, it was more of a belt than a dress now.

"God*damn*, you're beautiful," Mitch breathed, pulling back from their kiss so he could gaze at her with hooded eyes, his hands reverently cupping her lace-covered breasts. Back arching under his attention, she presented herself to him more fully and watched in fascination as he pushed the bra cups down and rolled her nipples between his thumb and forefingers.

"Oh my god!" her head flung back in abandon. This was beyond any pleasure she'd ever known. He dropped his head and warm lips mouthed at a nipple before his tongue circled it, laved it, drew it into his mouth. She could feel the sensation all the way down to her throbbing clit.

Forsaking her hold on his shoulders, she gripped onto his head, threading her fingers through his hair and holding his mouth to her. With his cheek stubble rasping deliciously against her sensitive skin, she wanted to scream with the pressure that was building inside.

She was grinding into the bulge of his cock searching for sweet relief, and it wasn't until his hand dropped to stroke the apex between her thighs that she jerked to a halt, excruciatingly aware of his hand cupping her slick need.

"You are so wet for me," he muttered into her neck, chasing the statement with the flat of his tongue licking up to her ear, "fuck that's hot."

Abruptly, Sara imagined the condemnation she would face from her parents if they saw her now. She remembered the images, of 16-year old her, plastered all over social media and the raging disappointment her parents had flayed her with.

Never mind she was a grown woman now and could have all the sex she wanted. She could imagine the potent disapproval her parents would slam her with over her choice of Mitch. She could feel their condemnation in her bones.

Pulling back from the abyss she was trembling on the precipice of, Sara struggled to regain a semblance of control. This was going *way* beyond what she was comfortable with. As desperate as her fevered skin was to have his touch – anywhere, everywhere – this was too much, too fast.

"Stop. Mitch, stop," she flattened her palms against his chest and pushed. Although her pressure was minimal, he immediately raised his head from the crook of her neck and stilled all movement.

"Sara? You okay?"

His voice was thick with lust and Sara almost gave in to temptation. Because my god he was so close and made her feel so good. So damn good.

"We need to slow it down."

"Okay, we can do that. Are you not… enjoying yourself?"

She gave him a little shove and rolled her eyes. "I think you know the answer to that, smartass."

With his free hand he held her chin so she had no choice but to hold his intent stare as he slowly withdrew his hand from between her legs. Dropping her eyes she watched him bring it to his mouth, open wide and suck his fingers in.

Oh yeah, she was *so* out of her depth here.

Alone in her apartment 20 minutes later, Sara was still on fire. She was actually getting concerned about the frantic rate of her heartbeat. Surely a little fooling around couldn't give you a heart attack?

Although lord knew it had been a little more than fooling around. With cold water running in the kitchen sink she splashed some on her heated cheeks and then cupped her hands to drink a few mouthfuls. Turning off the tap she didn't bother to dry her dripping face and instead snagged a stray hairband from the counter, twisting her long hair up into a messy bun.

Deep breath.

Mitch had let her go with a knowing smirk and a promise to be in touch to finish the interview. And other things.

Her insides felt fluttery and more than a bit panicked. She needed to talk to Sophie. Stat.

As she hit her best friend's phone number she sank into the couch, drawing her knees up and resting her chin on them. She needed advice that only Sophie could provide, because she was the only other person in the world who knew this particular little secret of Sara's.

"Sar! Hi!" Sophie's voice came over the phone distorted by background noise.

"Where are you?"

"I'm at the cattle yards with Robert. Hang on, I'll go and jump in the ute so I can hear you better."

Glancing at her watch, Sara wondered why they were doing cattle work when it was almost six o'clock on a Friday evening. Sophie's social calendar sure had changed since she'd moved to the country.

"Okay, I'm back! You want to know which shoes best match your outfit, right?"

Maybe my social life is changing too…

"Nope, I'm staying in tonight."

"Really? Since when does Sara Morrison miss after work drinks on a Friday? It's prime Husband Catching time." Sophie's voice was light, but Sara could detect an element of concern. "What happened with Phil?"

Why is everyone *asking about Phil?*

"Forget Phil. It's about that other guy I mentioned, the one I'm interviewing?"

"The douchebag?"

"Yeah, although it turns out he's not a complete dick. I met with him this afternoon and, I guess I kind of like him. He's really smart, actually."

"And hot. Don't forget you told me he was hot."

"Yeah, and hot," Sara exhaled. "And we kissed. Like, got down and dirty with each other's mouths."

"What!? Tell me *everything*," Sophie squealed.

"There's nothing else to tell, because then I freaked out and left."

"Because you wanted to stop, or because you wanted more?"

Yep, Sophie wasn't her best friend for nothing.

Over the silence she heard Sophie give a little sigh.

"Come on Sar. What's the problem?"

"You know what the problem is."

"It's not a problem honey, it's just a little anomaly that you'll fix when you're good and ready."

"It's not a little anomaly Soph, it's my virginity."

———

Well that had escalated fast. Mitch couldn't wipe the grin off his face.

He was stretched out on a lounger on his outdoor terrace, drinking a Corona and watching deep purple storm clouds descend over Bondi beach. The waves were white-capped and viciously pummeling the sand, tourists and locals alike heeding the approaching storm and deserting, leaving the stretch of sand uncommonly empty.

Mitch inhaled the distinctive scent of impending rain and settled a bent arm behind his head, watching as the late afternoon sky turned prematurely dark. Thunderstorms had unsettled him as a kid, but now the flashing lightning across the sky invigorated him.

Hell, who was he kidding? It wasn't Mother Nature that was shooting electricity through his synapses. It was a certain blonde princess, with interchangeable eye colour and the prettiest mouth he'd ever tasted. Just remembering the way her lips had parted on a breathy sigh, inviting his tongue to delve deeper into her sweetness, had him hot.

Sitting upright, he swung his legs over the side of the lounger and placed the beer bottle on the ground at his feet. He couldn't think of her and remain still. His chest was tight with *wanting* and his blood was heated. She was like a drug that had invaded his oxygen-deprived veins, seeping towards his heart to make it pump double time.

She was sassy and smart, and the way her nose crinkled when she laughed made his arms ache to pull her close. He wanted to be the reason her nose crinkled on a daily basis.

Pulling out his phone he tapped out a text message to her. He'd promised he'd be in contact. Who cared if that was only an hour ago?

Mitch: You okay? You left quickly.

Her response was gratifyingly quick.

Sara: Sorry. Freaked out a bit.
Mitch: About?
Sara: It just happened so fast. I'm not usually that unreserved.

Mitch chuckled out loud. Unreserved? Man, the woman had fallen apart in his arms. She'd been passionate and needy and abso-fucking-lutely incredible.

Mitch: Unreserved is an interesting choice of word. You've got to admit we have mad chemistry together.

He paced the length of the deck and then strode inside to the kitchen, throwing his empty beer bottle into the recycling bin before grabbing another from the fridge. As the minutes edged by without a response he cursed himself.

Damn. I'm coming on too strong.

He just didn't seem to be able to help himself when it came to her.

When the new message alert finally popped up on the screen, he fumbled with the phone in his haste to open it.

She has me on a string and doesn't even know it.

Sara: I admit nothing. But I need to see you again to finish the interview.
Mitch: Tomorrow?
Sara: What do you have in mind?
Mitch: Meet me out the front of Ink Inc. at 9am. Wear jeans.
Sara: Okaaaaay...
Mitch: Night Princess.
Sara: Sweet dreams.

"Fuuuuuck," he breathed out roughly. There was going to be nothing sweet about his dreams tonight.

If Ruby was the apple of Mitch's eye, then his custom 2008 Triumph Bonneville motorcycle came a very close second. It was attitude on two wheels, and looked poised to shred rubber, even when standing still.

With his helmet under his arm he leaned casually against it, watching Bondi as it geared up for a cruisy Saturday morning. A couple sipping takeaway coffees wandered past, their spare hands in each other's back pockets, a chocolate Labrador loping at their heels.

Mitch had *never* looked at someone else's relationship with interest, let alone envy. But there was definitely a touch of both as his eyes followed them. Up until his recent return to Australia, he'd had a new girlfriend every other week. But a real relationship? Hell, he didn't think he'd ever had one of those.

He'd told himself it was because he didn't believe in 'the one'. He'd scoffed at the idea of having a soul mate. When beautiful women threw themselves at you on a daily basis, it was easier to focus on lust than it was to think about love.

As crass as it was, women had become disposable to Mitch. It felt imperative that he hold them at arms length and not get too close. Not that he ever felt that he'd used them; the women he'd been with knew the score and he ensured they always had a mind-blowingly good time. He had a reputation to live up to, after all.

Why did all that seem so empty now?

The answer came sauntering up to him, long legs encased in sinfully tight jeans showcasing an *exceptional* ass and a loose white singlet showing calculated flashes of black lace bra beneath.

Sara was a walking wet dream.

"A motorbike?" she pushed her aviator sunglasses up and perused the Triumph with appreciative eyes, flashing a grin at him that near stopped his heart.

He'd wondered what the princess would think about riding on the back of his bike, and his decision to use it today was just as much about pushing her boundaries as it was about wanting her arms wrapped around his waist as he tore up the bitumen.

Turned out she was happy to push her own boundaries.

"Have you ridden before?" he picked up the spare helmet that sat on the seat of the bike and held it out to her.

"Do I look like I've ridden a motorcycle before?" she tipped her head up to him and raised her eyebrows playfully.

"My parents would have a *fit* at just the thought. But I'm game."

Hell yes she was. He'd been thrown when she'd slowed things down yesterday. Not a single woman he'd ever been with had thought he moved too fast. Frankly, most couldn't drop their panties fast enough.

But if he'd worried that Sara was pulling away before they'd even started, her eagerness now eased his concerns.

"Okay then."

Her hair hung over her shoulder in an intricate braid and he tugged on it gently, pulling her up against his muscled front until the helmet she held was pressed between them. Leaning down he brushed his lips against hers, which parted invitingly on a soft sigh. He was tempted, *so* tempted to take her up on the implied offer and deepen the kiss. Pressing their lips together hard and plundering her with his tongue.

But he could respect her need to take it slow. Swallowing a groan he pulled back, even as his cock stirred when she bit down on that full lower lip, her eyes lust dazed.

If she could look so delicious after a simple brushing of their lips, he was *dying* to know how she'd look in the throes of wild, passionate sex. And it would be wild and passionate; the chemistry they shared meant her body was made to be taken by his.

"Let me help you with that," he said, reaching for the open-faced helmet and helping her put it on, tightening the chinstrap.

"Should I ask where we're going?"

Her eyes – an aquamarine blue – were flashing with excitement.

"Does it matter?"

"Not really."

He grinned, putting on his own helmet and swinging a leg over the bike, kicking up the stand and revving it to life.

"Hop on."

Seeing Sara swing a leg over to straddle his bike, her arms catching around his waist, had him semi-aroused in seconds. God*damn* she was sexy.

"Hold on tight Princess."

CHAPTER 7

Sara was flying. And the only thing grounding her was the hot hardness of Mitch's torso that her arms were wrapped around. Between the man before her and the reverberations of his bike between her legs, she was at fever pitch.

The exhilaration of riding this thrumming machine down the streets of Sydney, zipping in and out of traffic with the wind rushing against her, had her believing she was a different person. One who didn't think about her parent's reactions before she got on the back of a motorcycle. She was a new woman.

Especially after her conversation with Sophie last night.

Mitch was the only man who had ever touched her like this. Ignited her like this. And she wanted her first time to be with him. She *knew* it would be amazing.

Like he said, they had 'mad chemistry'.

He'd promised a no-strings physical encounter, so she could ditch her virginity – in spectacular fashion – and then go back to her search for Mr Right. Easy.

Sophie had cautioned it might not actually be that easy, and told her she should tell Mitch she was a virgin. But she *really* didn't want to have that conversation. Better just to wing it, and see if she could fake it 'til she made it.

Sure as hell was working so far.

Sitting tight against his strong back she leaned with him as he took the bike around a corner, and then slowed. She bit back a protest. She didn't want this ride to end.

Laying her cheek against his broad expanse she clung tighter as he rolled the bike to a stop and quit the engine. The silence after the roar of the engine was shocking, as was the loss of vibrating sensation.

"Time to get off Princess," he said, his legs braced on the ground holding the bike upright.

Reluctantly she slid from the bike, pulling off her helmet as he followed suit and kicked the stand out to lean the bike against.

"I didn't ever understand the whole *Sons of Anarchy* phenomenon, but after that, I totally get it." She knew her cheeks were flushed from the wind and her excitement, and they heated further as Mitch placed big hands on her hips and tugged her up against him.

Goosebumps spread along her arms as his hands slipped beneath her top to rest against her bare waist, the calloused pads of his thumbs rubbing lazy circles on her skin.

It was electrifying.

This nearness to him, the *smell* of him, was making her dizzy. Looking up into his face – that chiseled jaw with day-old stubble hiding a dimple, those stunning blue eyes that simmered with a heat she knew reflected her own – she marveled at the clawing *need* that had claimed her.

"Uncle Mitch! You came!" trilled a little girl, bounding over in a pink tutu and ballet shoes.

Sara stepped quickly back, dropping hands that she belatedly realized had been clutching at Mitch's shirt.

Uncle Mitch?

Glancing around, Sara realized they'd pulled into the parking lot of a community hall, which was filling with cars that unloaded similarly attired small girls.

And was that? Oh Christ, it was the woman she'd seen with Mitch, the one who'd been wearing surgical scrubs. She was walking over, smiling as Mitch hoisted the little girl into his arms.

"We weren't sure if you'd make it. I told Ruby not to get her hopes up," said the woman, speaking to Mitch but openly giving Sara the onceover as she came to stand beside them. She wasn't unfriendly, but she was certainly guarded. Mitch's sister?

"As if I'd miss Apple's first ballet lesson. She's only been talking about it non-stop for the last week."

"And you bought company…" this time her gaze narrowed. "Even though we've spoken about not bringing your women around Ruby."

Sara winced. That stung.

"Maggie, this is Sara. And she's not just some woman." His tone had taken on an edge of warning. "She's interviewing me for a magazine, and I'm giving her some background context."

"Mmm hmm." She was unconvinced but stuck her hand out towards Sara. "I'm Maggie, Mitch's sister. And this is Ruby, my daughter."

"It's nice to meet you Maggie," Sara murmured, extending her own hand that Maggie squeezed gently before dropping. "And it's lovely to meet you Ruby, she look like a proper ballerina."

Ruby frowned down at her from Mitch's arms. "I *am* a proper ballerina. See my shoes?" She kicked her chubby legs out and pointed her toes.

"You absolutely are," Sara corrected herself with a quick

grin at Maggie. "Do you know how to stand in first position?"

"Show me," Ruby demanded as Mitch set her back on the ground.

Falling back on her years of classical ballet training, Sara easily transitioned her body into the simple, supple lines of first position, her arms graceful as they came to rest before her.

"Uncle Mitch, your woman is a ballerina!" Ruby breathed in wonder.

"Apple! She is not my woman, and that's not a polite thing to say," laughed Mitch.

"Apple?" asked Sara.

"Of my eye," he grinned back.

Well. This was definitely not the morning Sara had envisioned when she'd first seen him leaning so nonchalantly against his motorcycle. The bad boy tattooed biker had morphed into an adoring uncle.

"Come on Ruby, your class is going to start in a minute," said Maggie, scooping up the little girl and heading for the hall. "Are you and your woman coming?" she threw over her shoulder with a smirk.

"Seems that smirk is a family trademark," Sara muttered.

"One you obviously find irresistible," he joked, placing an arm over the top of her shoulders and drawing her tight against him. "Are you up for this? Watching a bunch of three-year olds dancing?"

"Sure. Ruby's as cute as a button. It's just… unexpected."

"You thought I was going to take you somewhere and ravish you?"

There was that smirk again.

"A girl can hope…" she fluttered her eyelashes

coquettishly.

This wasn't just flirting. She honest to god was ready for some ravishment. Her body had never been so primed in her life. She imagined her current high was similar to that achieved by taking illicit drugs.

Lord knew this was probably just as dangerous.

"All in good time," he breathed into her ear, leading them into the hall. "I seem to remember I need to make good on a promise to make you blush all over."

Her cheeks heated instantly.

Watching the little girls giggle and flounce around in their tutus was surprisingly nostalgic for Sara, who couldn't help but think of her own three-year old self taking ballet lessons. It had been fun, and her mum was always on the sidelines – encouraging and laughing.

It was good to remember her mother that way. She hadn't always been so focused on molding Sara into her "perfect" self.

Besides, she knew her mother's recent obsession with finding someone for Sara to settle down with came from a place of love; she just wanted her only child to be happy, to find the kind of loving relationship that she'd shared with Sara's father for 25 years.

It didn't help that Sara subscribed to the same fairytale herself.

And while Mitch may not be her knight in shining armour, he was nothing if not dashing and handsome. And damn if it didn't melt her to watch him around his niece.

As the lesson finished and they walked outside, a pirouetting Ruby ahead of them, Maggie maneuvered herself beside Sara as Mitch strode ahead, swinging Ruby over his shoulder.

"So you're writing a story about my big brother?" she asked, faux casually.

"Uh huh. You must be proud of the success he's achieved," Sara answered.

"I am. I hope you can look past his annoying arrogance and see the real man." Maggie put a hand on Sara's arm, urging her to a stop. "He left his career behind in the States to come home for Ruby and I, no questions asked. Family is everything to him, you know? And not just blood family, because it's just the three of us. He's got a way about him, of drawing people in and making them family too. Like Simon, and Jennifer. You know he made her a full business partner even though she couldn't bring any money into the arrangement? He's good people," she finished softly.

Sara bit her lip, not sure how to respond.

"Any blind fool can see there's more than the interview going on here. You're different. Not his usual type. Take it easy with him, okay?" Maggie's direct gaze didn't drop until Sara nodded.

"Okay. I think you'll be good for him."

Catching up with Mitch and Ruby, Maggie bundled Ruby into the car and turned to Mitch. "We're heading to the Blue Mountains to stay with Corinne for the weekend. I've got an afternoon shift on Monday, so we'll come back Monday morning." She looked at Sara and then back at her brother. "Don't do anything I wouldn't do."

"Seeing as you have a three-year old child…" drawled Mitch.

Maggie smacked him on the arm and got into the car, waving at them as she drove off.

"So I was going to take you for a scenic ride, but seeing as we have the apartment to ourselves, I say we head back to Bondi," he said.

Sara's heartbeat quickened. She seconded that.

"You live with Maggie and Ruby?"

"Yeah. I guess that's why I wanted you to meet them. You asked what drives my career, and it's them. Maggie and I had it tough, growing up. And now she's going through a rough patch so I came back to help her out. Her and Ruby are the only family I have, and succeeding in my career means we have security."

He dragged a hand roughly through his hair, his expression rueful.

"Hell, I'm not really sure why I wanted you to come today. I guess just to see me out of context, to get context. Does that make sense?"

"Perfectly."

"Well you're the journalist. I'm going to leave it in your capable hands."

"Let's stop talking and get riding. You're meant to be ravishing me, remember?"

———

Mitch didn't take women back to his home. Ever. So the fact he was now leading Sara into his apartment was kind of staggering. And had him strangely edgy.

"So, this is it," he waved a distracted hand to encompass the interior, while not taking his eyes off Sara. It suddenly mattered – a lot – what she thought.

He may be a street boy done good, but no amount of money or fame changed his upbringing and he knew he'd never be the kind of man Sara would take home to her parents.

What he *could* be was the man to give her the physical experience she was craving.

"This is seriously amazing. I don't even know what to say. It's stunning." She was turning in a slow circle, taking in the breathtaking north-easterly panorama across Bondi Beach.

Still with eyes only for her, he responded; "It is stunning, I'll give you that."

She was attuned to him like no woman ever had been and his rumbled, low voice had her coming to a stop in front of him.

"You're not bad yourself, Mitch Smith."

His throat was unexpectedly dry and all his practiced, smooth moves deserted him. He stood before her, feeling naked even while fully clothed.

She'd never have thought that if she knew the things he'd done in his past.

"I didn't really expect to, you know, *like* you," she admitted with a tiny smile, running her fingers lightly up his forearm. "I thought you were such a jerk when I first met you."

"I am a jerk, you shouldn't forget that."

"You cultivate the image of a jerk, but I think you're hiding a good guy behind all that bravado."

"Do you have a psychology degree I don't know about?"

Those fingers of hers were still lightly stroking the lines of ink on his arm, and he could feel it deep in his balls. He was going to combust if he didn't have her. Soon.

"Nope, but I've been on a lot of dates. I'm an expert on men and their personalities."

The thought of her with other men did a number on his brain. He had an actual physical reaction, with his muscles tensing and his stomach dropping. He wanted to wipe all memory of every man who had come before him. He wanted his face, his body, his touch to be the only ones Sara remembered.

A growl reverberated from his chest and her fingers stilled.

"That came out wrong. I don't want you to think I'm, like, loose, or anything."

He was at a loss as to what to say to that. He'd never once thought she was loose. And hell, it's not like he was in a position to judge anyone. She was 24-years old and outrageously beautiful, of course she was going to have had men in her past. All that mattered was that he was her present.

The ringing of his phone saved him from a response, and he reached into his back pocket for it.

"Hang on, let me check it's not Maggie calling. She just got her rust bucket car back from the mechanics and I wouldn't be surprised if it decides to die on the side of the road somewhere..."

The number was unfamiliar, but he'd had a missed call from it a couple of days ago. Whoever it was hadn't left a message, and he wasn't inclined to find out right now who it could be. They could leave a message. Or not. He had more pressing matters to attend to.

Tossing the phone onto the low-slung coffee table he advanced on Sara, who had retreated to the wall of floor-to-ceiling windows and was twisting her hands together, gazing out.

"I don't think you're loose Sara, I think you're perfect," he whispered roughly into her ear, running his hands up her arms and drawing her back against his chest. "Way too good for me, but I'm going to take what I can get with you."

His teeth nipped at her earlobe and then he moved lower, nuzzling his face into the smooth skin of her neck, inhaling deep. He realized, with stunning clarity, that he was falling for this woman. This woman who was so far out of his reach it was laughable.

He didn't know when it had happened. *How* it had happened. And he wasn't sure he liked the crazy, blood-rushing feverish high that accompanied it; he was out of control.

"So kiss me. Take me," she breathed, turning in his arms and rising on tiptoe. She pulled his head down to meet her lips and he willingly submitted, cupping her ass in his hands to bring her higher. Closer.

Although he could feel her pulsing with need she was tentative, slowly gliding her tongue over his lips, pulling back when he opened for her and sucking instead on his lower lip. He was desperate to fuse their mouths, to taste her, to claim her. But she wanted slow and he was taking his cues from her.

He kneaded her ass, fervently wishing he hadn't dictated she wear jeans. If she'd been in a dress, he could have pushed the material of her panties aside and been stroking her bare flesh. Could have run his hands down and dipped between to caress her intimate wetness…

His hips involuntarily bucked into her, the bulge of his erection pressing against her stomach. He was as worked up as a schoolboy.

Reacting to his pounding lust, she released his sweetly tortured bottom lip and licked into his mouth. He couldn't hold back. With a groan he plundered her open lips, thrusting his tongue against hers in an erotic tease of what was to come.

He needed his cock sheathed in her. He wanted to be rocking in and out of her as she thrashed her head in pleasure and gasped his name. *Screamed* his name.

Panting heavily, he pulled back.

Slow it down, slow it down.

He didn't want to scare her off again.

"Are we doing this?" he asked, searching her heavy-lidded eyes.

"Yes. Now."

There was a determination to her words that surprised him. Her eyes sharpened with intent as she deliberately reached for his straining erection, rubbing it through the denim of his jeans. But there was a telltale tremble to her hand and a naive uncertainty that threw him. Something was off.

She wanted to take charge, but she was tentative. She wanted to go slow but she wanted it now.

Circling both her wrists with his hands he stilled her movement, bringing their clasped hands to rest between their bodies, over his galloping heart.

"Sara, what are you thinking? Where's your head at?"

"We're not thinking Mitch, we're doing. And I thought I was going to be doing you."

She pulled her hands from his and tried to step back, but the wall of glass had her hemmed in. In a bid to hide the shaking of her hands she propped them on her hips, glaring at him defiantly.

Woah. That went to shit real quick.

"Okay Princess, take it easy. I just need to be sure that this is definitely what you want, that you're comfortable with what's happening."

"I do, I do want this. Just fuck me already."

"So yeah, now I *know* there's a problem. This isn't you Sara."

"What the hell do you know about me? You promised me an experience I wouldn't forget, remember? And that's what I want."

"Not like this, babe. You're angry. Don't get me wrong, I like it when you're assertive, but just – not like this."

"What? I'm not enough of a bimbo? My boobs aren't big enough? Want me on my knees blowing you?"

Her voice cracked.

And his heart cracked. He didn't know what was wrong, but something sure as fuck was.

Bending, he reached and caught behind her knees, lifting to cradle her in his arms. She struggled half-heartedly to get free but he held firm, striding across the living space and into his bedroom.

Still holding her, he settled on the mattress against the bedhead with her now limp body supported between his chest and bent knees. He had absolutely no idea what was going on, but he murmured reassurances into her hair as she nestled into his chest, her tears wetting his shirt.

When her shoulders finally stopped shaking and her breathing evened out, he framed her face with his hands and tilted her head up. Her eyelashes were spiky with tears and her eyes couldn't meet his.

"Sara, what's going on?" He kept his voice gentle, but his pulse was racing. He was so far out of his depth here.

"I'm sorry. This isn't what you signed up for." She gave a wry grimace and wiped at her cheeks; "I'm a mess."

"You're not answering my question babe."

"Look, it doesn't matter," she attempted to dislodge herself from his lap, but he held tighter. She wasn't going anywhere until he got a handle on what was happening.

Her eyes flashed to him and he was reassured to see the spirit he'd come to associate with her. They could work through this.

"Seriously Mitch, let's just notch this up as the failure it is, and call it quits."

"I am *not* calling it quits on you Sara."

Sighing, she brushed a single finger over his lips.

"You could have any woman you want, you don't need to mess with me."

"I want to mess with you."

"Look, I should have been upfront with you earlier, and saved you the time. I'm not like the women you're usually with –"

"Don't you think I don't know that?" he interrupted.

"Mitch, I'm a virgin."

CHAPTER 8

Sara felt his whole body stiffen beneath her. His hands, which had been stroking up and down her arms, stilled.

This whole situation was ridiculous. Had she really thought that this sexy, charismatic man – who could have his pick of women – would want to mess around with her? She already knew she wasn't his type, so why on earth had she felt the need to confirm that by spilling her guts about her virginity?

I should have trusted my first instinct and stayed far, far away.

But she was lying to herself. Her very first instinct when she'd met Mitch was to rip his clothes off; the primal magnetism that flashed between them had bypassed her usual reservation and, dear god, she'd wanted him. Fiercely.

And now? She wanted to know the intimacy of having sex with a man. Of having sex with *him*. The all-encompassing desire was such that she honestly didn't care what her parents would think. She *wanted* this.

With her heart caught in her throat, she stared at her clasped hands in her lap and waited for him to speak. When he didn't she sucked in a breath. He'd been saying all the right things, making all the right moves, and she knew it wasn't just because he wanted into her panties. He was a good man.

Just obviously not up to handling the revelation of her lack of sexual experience.

"I'm sorry," she muttered softly, not raising her eyes. "I thought I was ready. I mean, I *am* ready, but I guess I just don't, you know, really know what I'm doing and I got nervous and was obviously, I guess, doing it wrong - "

Before she could finish her rambling sentence his large hand cupped the side of her face and tilted her head up, his intent eyes snagging her own.

She blinked.

"You weren't doing anything *wrong* Sara, it just didn't feel right. I didn't know what was going on in that head of yours, and it worried me." He tapped a gentle finger against her temple.

"Obviously I was doing it wrong if you were thinking about my head, and not my body," she said, dropping her eyes in embarrassment, frustrated at her lack of carnal knowledge.

This was clearly what Sophie had alluded to when she cautioned losing her virginity may not be as easy as she'd thought.

Jesus. What 24-year old is still a virgin?

Her skin was overheated and she desperately wanted to put some distance between her and the man whose chest she was currently cradled against.

She wriggled from his lap and stood, but before she could move away he'd swung his legs off the side of the bed and caught her hand in both his large ones.

"Wait, Sara. I want to talk about this."

She raised her eyebrow and gave a half-hearted smirk. "Talk? Careful Mitch, that man-whore reputation of yours is getting trashed."

He didn't smile, just rose slowly from the bed so he was looming over her, crowding her personal space. She took a step back and he took another forward, shadowing her.

"It's not my past I think we need to discuss Sara, it's yours." His voice was a deep, silky rumble and penetrated straight past any emotional defenses she thought she'd constructed.

"Your *past*? As in, you don't consider yourself a man-whore any longer?" Sara's pulse spiked. "What are you telling me?"

A small part of her was still anxious to escape. To burrow into her bed and spoon ice-cream straight from the tub. To forget this encounter and the fact that she'd tried, and failed, to lose her virginity. At 24.

I am so *embarrassed.*

But a larger part of her was transfixed by this man. By his effect on her.

The rush of endorphins she felt whenever he was near was intoxicating and, while it was possibly hindering her better judgment, it was so addictive she was beyond caring.

"I haven't been with anyone else since I met you, and I've never brought a woman to my home before." His words were slow and measured, as though he didn't want her to miss a single one.

Her face must have registered surprise and skepticism, because he repeated himself.

"No one since I met you Sara."

It wasn't lost on her that since her attempted seduction had floundered into a mini-breakdown, he hadn't once called her Princess. His repeated use of her name, rather than the nickname he'd given her, was a balm on her confused awkwardness.

She wished like hell she had even an ounce of the sexual confidence she imagined his previous lovers had in spades.

It grated that in all other aspects of her life she had her shit together but when it came to sex she didn't even *know* what she didn't know.

And she wanted Mitch to be the one to teach her.

"So do you still want to? Have sex?" She was proud that her voice didn't betray just how unsure she was right now. Her nervousness had totally ruined the moment before – she needed to project assurance if this was going to happen.

"I don't want to just have sex with you Sara." His sensuous lips curled up in a predatory smile as his hand wrapped around the back of her neck and pulled her into his Viking body, his head dropping to whisper at her ear.

"I want to devour you. It's not going to be sex, it's going to be communion." His teeth grazed her earlobe before his lips were moving down her neck, causing ripples of shivers to chase each other down her back.

"I am going to worship your body in a way that goes so far beyond sex, you're not going to know what's hit you."

If he hadn't been holding onto her elbows as he hotly promised this against her skin, she may well have fainted with the sheer perfection of his words. The man standing before her was so far removed from what she'd originally thought him to be.

He was more than the ink on his skin, the flash of his dimple or his hard muscle-sculpted body. More than the reckless and carefree demeanor he portrayed, and definitely more than his public persona of a womanizing playboy.

He was nothing that she thought she was looking for in a man, but hell if he wasn't getting to her.

"So that's a yes then?" she murmured, leaning into his chest and inhaling the husky maleness of him. It was a scent that was literally making her weak at the knees.

Pressing an open-mouthed kiss to her neck he pulled his head up and, using the hands that were still grasping her elbows, set her back from him.

She instantly missed the nearness of him. The heat.

"Yes, Princess, that's a yes. But first, we talk."

She resisted the urge to roll her eyes and instead gave an exaggerated pout. He'd basically used his words as foreplay, promising her the world, and now he wanted to *talk*? She was definitely doing something wrong here.

"The fact that I'm a virgin doesn't have to change anything."

"Sara, it changes *everything*. If I hadn't realized something was wrong, and we'd kept going, your first time would have been right there in my lounge room."

"And that's a problem why?"

"Because your first time shouldn't be hard and fast against a wall."

"It should be special?" she gently mocked, softening the words with a smile. "Come on Mitch, I want you, you want me. Let's just have some fun."

"Oh it'll be fun alright," he growled, stepping forward to hoist her up into a fireman's hold over his shoulder and marching with her out of the bedroom.

Sara squealed with surprise and then giggled, stopping only when she realized how *cute* she sounded. Cute wasn't going to get Mitch Smith into bed. She needed him to see her for the woman she was.

He dropped her softly onto the sofa and settled beside her, although with far too much distance between them for her liking.

"Do you want a drink?"

"I want you."

"*Damn* woman," he dragged a hand through his hair and dropped his elbows to his knees, his head hanging. "I am trying *really* hard to do the right thing here."

"There's only one thing I want *really hard* right now," she purred, loving that he was struggling. It was a relief that he still wanted her, even knowing what he was dealing with.

Without looking at her he sprang to his feet and headed for the kitchen, coming back with two glasses of water and a noticeably calmer expression.

"Sara, talk to me. How does an intelligent and beautiful woman like you get to your age and still have your virginity? I struggle to understand the fact you're single, let alone finding out you're virtually untouched. It blows my mind."

"Blows your mind in a bad way?"

"Blows my mind in that I can't believe the male population of this city must be the dumbest fuckers alive. Blows my mind that you think *I* should be the person you want to do this with. I mean Jesus Sara, this is a pretty big deal, and not just for you. I haven't ever had sex with a virgin before. I feel like I should Google what to do."

Choking on the mouthful of water she'd just swallowed, Sara couldn't stop a delighted smile spreading across her face.

"I'm pretty sure you can handle this without the help of Google."

———

The grin that graced Sara's face set Mitch somewhat at ease, although his body was still jacked and his mind reeling. The strength of his feelings for her had thrown him for a loop *before* she'd dropped the bombshell of her virginity. Now? Hell, he needed a scotch on the rocks to help him through this.

He'd known from the very start that he wasn't good enough to be with a woman like Sara. Knew he should leave well enough alone. But the temptation of just *once* with her had been too much. And now to know he was going to be her first? He was surprised he wasn't beating on his chest caveman-style.

"Help me out here Sara. How on earth are you still a virgin? Did your parents lock you up as a teenager and only just let you out?"

He could not fathom how Sara – stunning, amazing Sara – had managed to keep men away. And, if he were honest, he was scared the answer was something he was going to lose his shit over. If she'd been abused in any way... his fists curled into themselves and his temples throbbed with each pump of blood through his body as he recalled a dark night when he did lose his shit. When he and Simon exacted justice for a wrong that should never have happened, and from that vengeance one kid ended up dead and another with jail time.

But here and now sure as hell wasn't the place to be dwelling on the past.

Sara ran the tip of her finger around the rim of her water glass, thinking over her response. He was glad she was at last taking his reserve seriously. This was a big fucking deal and he needed to know the how and the why.

Her braided hair was coming loose and tumbling over her shoulders and she pushed it away while straightening her posture and meeting his gaze.

"When I was sixteen I was dating a guy – he'd been my boyfriend for about six months when we decided we were ready to take things further," she took a quick sip of her water. "So we tried to, uh, have sex, but it didn't really work and was painful and so we stopped. But then he went and told all his friends that we'd done it and had some photos of me on his phone that he flashed around. When I broke up with him because of that, he spread it around that I was a slut and that we'd done all kinds of things that we hadn't, and then the photos ended up on social media and they just wouldn't *go away*."

Mitch had to place his water glass on the coffee table because he was worried it was going to shatter into pieces in his hand.

What a fucking piece of shit.

"What was his name?" he grunted the question because his throat felt like a boulder was wedged down it.

"It doesn't matter. The point is, after that I got asked out a lot, like *a lot*. But it was just guys who'd heard that I was easy and wanted to get laid. And I just said no to everyone. Not that my parents would have let me date, when they found out they totally lost it and made me promise I'd wait until I was married," she gave a small eye roll. "They were worried that no boy from a nice family would marry me with a sullied reputation."

Mitch's dentist was going to give him grief over the state of his molars.

"I was so ashamed about the reputation I'd been given that I pretty much stopped even talking to guys. And then by the time I got to college and left that all behind, I didn't know how to tell a guy that I was still a virgin. It was embarrassing, I mean, *no one* was a virgin at college. And so it was easier to just break it off with a guy before it got to the point of things going any further."

Mitch had so much respect for the fact that Sara had maintained eye contact with him the whole time she was talking. The telling of this obviously wasn't easy for her – hell, it wasn't easy to hear. It killed him to think of how vicious teenagers could be, and how it was still affecting her now.

"I'm assuming this isn't well known? Otherwise there'd be an urban myth about the crazy beautiful woman who was still a virgin, and Sydney men would be going wild to get their hands on you," he asked wryly.

"No, the only other person I've ever told is my best friend Sophie. And it's not like I haven't been dating, I've just been waiting for – god, I don't really know what I've been waiting for," she admitted.

"Me," he asserted. "Tension and desire, remember?"

"You have *got* to stop bringing that conversation up!" She threw a cushion at him. "And don't get a big head, who says I think we have tension and desire?"

"You might want to Princess, but you can't deny the chemistry we have," he drawled, leaning across and capturing those luscious lips of hers in a lingering kiss.

Even he didn't know the last time he'd felt this much tension and desire with a woman, if ever.

Shifting, he positioned himself over her and pushed her back onto the sofa, bringing them flush against each other and reveling in how right it felt to cover her small body with his own. Dipping to claim her lips again, he couldn't help his smile curving against her mouth as she mewled in pleasure.

The noises she made had his whole body throbbing.

Having felt his grin she swatted the back of his head and spoke against his questing lips; "Okay, I admit there's tension and desire. There's no need to gloat about it."

He didn't respond, just deepened the kiss. She was the sweetest thing he'd ever tasted, and he couldn't get enough. Couldn't get close enough.

Even as his body roared to consummate the passion between them, he knew he needed to pull back. He was going to take it slow and careful, and not just because of her untried state. He was selfish enough to admit once wasn't going to be enough with her and, by dragging this experience out, he'd get to spend more time with her.

He knew with absolute certainty that she was too good for him. That he should let her go. He wasn't worthy of taking her virginity. He wasn't worthy of being with her full stop. But *Jesus*, knowing that no other man had ever given her the pleasure he knew he could was intoxicating. In this moment, she was absolutely his.

He'd wanted to wipe all memory of every man who'd come before him, but now his body and his touch would be the only ones Sara had known. The knowledge was enough to make him blow his load right here, right now.

Kissing his way hotly down her neck he pushed her singlet up and used his lips to traverse the softness of her stomach, noting her thighs clenching together in tension. He tugged the singlet up and over her head, Sara raising her arms obediently, allowing him to pull the garment free.

God, if he weren't already horizontal, the sight of her in that black lace bra would have brought him to his knees. The swell of her breasts pushed tantalizingly over the lace cups, which couldn't disguise hard pebbled nipples that had him salivating.

Flicking the catch at the front of her bra he bared her to his starved gaze, his mouth descending on first one taut nipple, and then the other, laving and worshipping them as his hands caressed the fullness of her breasts.

"*Mitch*." Sara's arms were still flung above her head from when he'd removed her singlet, and with her eyes closed in abandon and her breathing choppy with lust, she was literally breathtaking – Mitch's chest was tight and he was struggling to draw enough oxygen into his lungs.

Rising back onto his haunches, he locked eyes with Sara who had opened hers to watch him as he undid the button on her jeans and then slowly, slowly pulled them down – her hips rising and wriggling in assistance.

When she was splayed before him in just her panties he paused, hungry eyes devouring every inch of her.

The primal urge to feel his skin on hers had him shucking his own shirt off, throwing it to the ground and feeling like an absolute *god* when her lips parted in a breathy sigh of appreciation – her eyes roaming his inked skin.

"God, Mitch, I'm *aching*. You need to do something," she implored, reaching for him and attempting to pull him down on top of her.

"We're not rushing this Sara," he warned, resisting her hands and capturing them in one of his to raise them back above her head.

"I'm ready, I promise I'm ready," she pleaded, breath panting and eyes feverish.

He ran a teasing hand lightly over the lace between the

apex of her thighs, which trembled as her hips rose into his touch.

"Yeah you're wet babe, but I want you soaking."

Turning her head into the sofa cushion she moaned, which had his erection pounding painfully behind the zipper of his jeans.

He was taking this slow, even if it killed him.

CHAPTER 9

Sara burned for Mitch's touch. If he didn't do something *right now* she was going to combust. Literally shatter into a thousand molten pieces.

A shameless, needy moan fell from her lips as he hauled her to sit up against his washboard abs; her legs stretched wide, straddling the girth of him.

Holy hell he was a big man.

As much as she wanted to explore the length and breadth of him, run her hands over every inch of his mouthwateringly inked skin, her needs were far beyond such pleasures.

Finding purchase against the sofa with her knees and gripping his shoulders for balance, she ground herself against the bulge of his erection. The seam of his jeans provided delicious friction to her over-heated core and she rocked feverishly, gasping his name.

His hands went behind to cup her ass, rhythmically squeezing and kneading, urging on her movements while his intense, hooded eyes stayed locked on her bare and swaying breasts.

Lost to the building pressure she tipped her head back, thrusting her chest out further, which Mitch took advantage of – dipping and capturing one puckered nipple between his teeth, tugging not-so-gently and causing a shiver of pain-edged pleasure to shoot straight to her throbbing clit.

Flexing her fingers into his shoulders she cried out in

abandon, pushing her pelvis down harder.

"Shhh, shhh, shhh," Mitch crooned in a rumble, using his grip on her ass to still her, holding her against his cock. "We're going slow, remember?"

Sara couldn't speak. She opened stunned eyes, staring at him in pent-up frustration.

Slow? He has to be freakin' kidding.

He smiled that charming, crooked smile of his and brought one hand around to run the tip of his middle finger down the center of Sara's nose.

"Yes Princess, slow," he answered her unasked question.

That finger of his continued its descent, blithely running between her sweat-sheened breasts and down lower to her abdomen, which clenched at the feather-light touch.

"I can't wait to feel the slick velvet of your pussy," he whispered hoarsely, the deepening timbre of his voice belying his own ratcheted-up need.

The effect of his dirty words was instantaneous. Sara was now soaking, just as he'd wanted. It was testament to how far gone she was that this didn't bother her in the slightest. Sitting astride him she felt beautiful, confident.

He shifted her slightly and slipped his hand inside her panties, pushing them aside so his finger could stroke through her intimate folds before slipping into her needy core.

"Oh yeah baby, you feel so good," he breathed in wonder, feathering kisses over her closed eyes before angling his lips over hers and kissing her senseless. Moaning as he sucked on her tongue she gave a first tentative tilt of her pelvis, moving against his penetrating finger.

Encouraged, he slid another finger in and she spread her thighs wider to accommodate him. The feeling of fullness was incredible and when his thumb swiped over the tender nub of her clit she gave an involuntary buck, pushing against his hand.

"Oh fuck. Mitch! This is - "

She inhaled sharply as he withdrew his fingers only to pump them back inside.

"It's what Princess?"

If she weren't so close to tumbling into oblivion, she'd be pissed at how he was keeping it together while she was falling apart in his arms.

Instead, she rode his fingers with circling hips, the spiraling force of pleasure building so that she was momentarily afraid she'd black out.

Gasping for air she was distracted by Mitch's dexterous thumb, thrumming her clit with an ever-increasing momentum. And when he crooked those two fingers inside her, hitting her sweet spot, an orgasm pounded over her – stars exploding behind her tight-shut eyes as her internal muscles clenched around his fingers. Heat streaked through her, blistering her synapses and leaving her crying his name as she fell against his chest, spent.

Heaving to catch her breath, her body continued its reflexive shuddering in the aftermath of her unraveling as Mitch's voice vibrated against her neck with reverent endearments.

His hands swept up and down her naked back, stroking and caressing.

Holy shit.

What he had done to her – the way he had made her feel – was almost beyond her comprehension. She hadn't even known her body was capable of such an earthshattering response.

"That was good, huh?" he teased, nudging her chin with his knuckles so he could see her face.

She turned her head to bite the thumb of the hand that was cradling her face, a cheeky smile tugging at the corners of her mouth.

"It was okay."

Smirking, he reclined his over-sized body down the length of the couch, one bent leg hanging off the side with a foot bracing against the floor and Sara draped across the broad expanse of his chest.

His jeans were riding low on his hips, and the tantalizing v of muscle leading into the waistband was driving her crazy because he kept removing her hands whenever she tried to venture south.

"I told you Princess, today was about you – not me. Trust me, we'll get to me, just not right now," he murmured against her mouth, capturing her bottom lip and sucking.

The weighty post-orgasm euphoria had Sara too languorous to disagree strongly. Her limbs were heavy and slack, her insides melted. She let her cheek rest against his perfectly defined pectoral and finally took the time to study the intricate tattoos covering his torso and running down his arms. Her fingers wandered, stroking the lines of ink and marveling at the pure artistry.

"Which was your first one?" she asked.

"My first tat?"

"Yeah, do you even remember?"

"Of course I remember. Just like you're going to remember yours, too."

Propping her chin on his chest she met his twinkling eyes,

giving a non-committal hum as she did so.

"It was this one," he said, pointing at a scroll of words that read 'my strength and my weakness' on his left bicep.

"My strength and my weakness? I'm assuming there's a story attached to that?"

"My family."

"Maggie?"

"And my mother. God we loved her. But she loved heroin more. In the end, my love for her made me weak, and I wasn't able to help her. Stop her. It was on my watch that she overdosed."

"Oh Mitch. I don't even have words. How old were you?"

"Sixteen. But that was a long time ago. And today isn't about me, remember? Tell me Princess, exactly how much of a virgin are you?"

"I didn't know there were degrees of virginity," she replied with a grin, allowing him to lighten the conversation.

"Well you're technically a virgin, because you haven't had sex with a man. But do you pleasure yourself?"

"That's a bit personal, isn't it?" she exclaimed, ducking her head down so she didn't have to meet his eyes.

"Considering what we just did, I think we're beyond embarrassment Sara," he chuckled. When she didn't respond, he prompted her; "So, do you pleasure yourself?"

"I'm a virgin, not a nun," she mumbled into his skin. "Of course I masturbate."

"With just your fingers, or do you use sex toys?"

"Seriously?" her head popped up again. "I don't see how that concerns you."

"Seeing as I *am* going to have sex with you Sara, it would be good to know how *accustomed* to penetration you are."

His emphasis on the word 'accustomed' had Sara squirming.

"Just fingers."

"See? That wasn't so bad to tell me, was it?" he cajoled, working his own fingers into Sara's tousled braid and rubbing her scalp.

She moaned a response. This man's hands were pure magic.

The sudden not-so-subtle rumble of her stomach disrupted the moment. It was now early afternoon, and she hadn't eaten since breakfast.

The magic fingers stopped their rubbing, and this time her moan was one of disapproval. She may well die if he stopped now, they felt *that* good.

He chuckled, sliding his hands out of her hair and bringing them to rest lightly on her shoulders.

"We seem to have skipped lunch Princess. How about I go and see what I've got in the fridge to make us some sandwiches?"

"Really? As a man-whore, you should know that in these situations, food is highly overrated. Want to know what would be so much more fun?" she pushed herself up and off his torso but remained straddling him, her fingers following that intriguing trail of hair that led from his belly to disappear beneath the waistband of his jeans.

"I don't know what could be more fun than ham and cheese," he deadpanned back at her.

"Not even this?" she asked, popping the button of his jeans and slipping a hand down to grasp his straining, ready cock through the material of his boxers. "Because I think this could be *really* fun."

Mitch growled long and low. She was literally going to be the death of him. His cock surged of its own volition into her eager hands and he clenched his buttocks against the natural inclination to rock into her. To pump his release all over her.

His throat was dry and it took two attempts to get his words out, and even then all he could manage was "Sara, *Jesus*."

The sight of her astride him, her bare breasts swaying as her hand stroked his shaft, her long blonde hair disheveled and her lush lips pursed in concentration was enough to drive a good man insane. And he was *not* a good man.

But damn it, he was trying to be.

Drawing on fast-dwindling levels of determination, he raised himself onto his elbows so he was at eye level with Sara, who was watching him with bright eyes.

"Babe, as much as I love having your hands down my pants, you have to stop."

"What? This?" she breathed, those fingers of hers slipping beneath his boxers and tightening around the base of his cock. Mesmerized, he watched as she then swept upwards to his engorged head, a shiny drop of pre-cum lubricating her downward stroke.

She was a vixen. A temptress. And she was seducing the hell out of him.

How the fuck *is she still a virgin?*

"You are going to drive me crazy woman," he groaned, resisting – barely – the urge to thrust his hips. "Seriously, Sar. Stop, please. For the love of God."

She just smiled wickedly at him and continued her ministrations. Until a phone rang, startling her into stilling.

"Is that yours or mine?" he asked.

"Who cares?"

She resumed her rhythmic stroking and Mitch's balls tightened. Jesus, was he going to come from just a hand job?

The phone started again, its insistent ringtone enough to haul Mitch out of his lust-filled haze.

Displacing her gently he got to his feet, buttoning his jeans over his throbbing cock and taking a deep breath. All his blood had headed south, and he was lightheaded at the sudden deprivation of Sara's touch.

"Sorry Princess. I need to check that it isn't Maggie stranded on the side of the road."

The ringing ceased as he strode over to the coffee table and snagged his phone, which showed a blank screen, but started up again as he turned around.

"It's yours," he said, picking up her handbag and bringing it over to her. "And whoever it is appears desperate to talk to you."

Sara was refastening her bra and pulling her singlet over her head and, even though Mitch knew it was for the best, he couldn't help lamenting the missed opportunity. She wriggled into her panties and then rummaged through her handbag to locate the phone, which was vibrating with what appeared to be several voice messages.

"Damn! I forgot I'm meeting with mum this afternoon," she moaned, her fingers tapping out a text message saying she was on her way.

"Are you late?" he asked, lifting the hair from her nape and pressing a kiss there before stepping back. Was it crazy to be missing her already?

"I'm going to be. It's just a meeting for some fancy black tie charity dinner. One of the committee members pulled out and mum has roped me in."

She stepped into her jeans and pulled them on as she listened to her voice message. The sight was almost as erotic as if she'd been taking them off.

She has totally done a number on me.

Mitch scrubbed a hand across his face and willed his erection to subside. Heading to the kitchen he grabbed one of Ruby's muesli bars and a banana, bringing them back to Sara who had finished gathering her belongings.

"Was there a problem?" He figured no one called repeatedly and in succession unless there was some kind of emergency.

"Nope. She just wants me to pick up some Roquefort from the deli on Queen Street on my way."

"Do I even want to know what Roquefort is?" he asked dryly.

"It's a blue cheese made from sheep's milk. French, I think. Apparently it's *imperative* for the cheese board mum is putting together. She's hosting the meeting and takes her job *very* seriously," Sara quipped.

"Here, take these. You must be starving – you can eat them on the way."

She took the proffered snacks and then stepped into him, winding her arms around his torso and tilting her head up to see his face.

"Sorry I have to run. Especially leaving you, uh, not finished."

He grinned down at her.

"Just means you owe me one. When can I see you again?"

"Can I call you? My head is all over the place, and I can't think what my schedule is like at the moment."

She must have seen the disappointment he tried to hide, because she pressed closer – the peaked tips of her breasts pushing into his bare chest.

"It'll be soon, Mitch. Promise."

With Maggie and Ruby gone for the weekend the apartment felt empty and, after a punishing weights session, Mitch was pumped and antsy. He was regretting turning down Simon's offer of a beer when his phone pinged with an incoming text message. But he nearly threw it in frustration when he saw it wasn't from the one person he wanted it to be.

But of course it wouldn't be Sara. She was busy at her committee meeting, for some posh charity event that would probably be attended by a hoard of suitable husband-material society dicks.

He opened the text message anyway, it was from the leggy brunette Mandy. There was no message with the text, just a photo of a very naked Mandy with her very fake breasts.

From a purely male perspective he could appreciate the image, but it didn't stir his blood. And it sure as hell didn't tempt him to reply to the message with an invitation to meet up, which was obviously Mandy's intention.

Besides which, now that he had his niece in his life he was not so blasé about naked selfies; he didn't want Ruby to grow up and think it was normal – or expected – for her to send compromising photos of herself to random men.

Still, he hesitated a beat before deleting the message.

Mandy had a banging body.

He wasn't entirely sure where these newfound morals had come from. He was mildly shocked that even though Sara had insisted she was ready, he'd called her out on it. And he was *definitely* anxious about the idea of being her first.

He was a ghetto boy from the streets of Western Sydney, covered in ink and reeking of attitude. And she was an Eastern Suburbs princess who oozed class and was looking for a husband.

Not exactly a match made in heaven.

He popped the top of a beer and took a long swallow, dropping onto the sofa with his legs spread wide and an arm thrown along the back. Resting the cool bottle of beer on his stomach he contemplated the day. He didn't know what to make of the fact that she hadn't commented when he revealed he hadn't been with anyone else since he'd met her. And she'd called him a man-whore. Twice.

He wasn't sure how he felt about that. In fact, the tangle of emotions running havoc inside him was confusing as hell. A serious case of blue balls wasn't helping.

He closed his eyes, remembering having his mouth on her and swallowing her feverish, throaty cries. Loving that her smell still lingered on his fingers.

Yep, he was in over his head with this one.

CHAPTER 10

"Soph tell me, how big is big?"

"What, like, his penis?"

Sara fell back onto the bed and clutched the phone tighter to her ear, wondering if she shouldn't just re-direct the conversation and forget her questions. She sighed.

"Yes, his penis. Although can we not call it a penis? It sounds like we're in biology class."

Sophie snorted into the phone and couldn't hold back a giggle.

"Sure Sar, what would you like to name it? Mr Big? Or what about Bed Snake? Excalibur?" She snorted again.

"Those snorts are just charming Sophie. I bet you don't do that in front of Robert."

"Oh please. I'm pregnant – all my dignity went out the window a long time ago. You wouldn't believe the excess gas I have these days."

"No! No. Please. I haven't even had sex, let's not turn me off the concept because I'm petrified of getting up the duff. So back to his cock –"

"Oh you little floozy! Jumping straight from penis to cock. I'm so proud of you right now."

"Sophie. Concentrate. I'm worried that it's so big it's not going to fit – can that happen?"

"Well, you know you can't really judge the size when it's flaccid…"

"That's another banned word. And I've only seen it erect. And huge. Seriously Soph, it's bigger than any vibrator I've ever seen."

There was more than a beat of silence.

"Okay, so I'm not going to tell you how lucky you are. One day when you're faced with a sub-par penis you're going to realize what a catch Mitch is. Right now, you just need to know that so long as he knows what he's doing with it, and you're uh, *ready* for it, then it should be fine."

Sara squirmed a little remembering just how *ready* she'd been yesterday. She wasn't clueless; she knew her body prepared itself when aroused. But dear God, the amount Mitch aroused her was almost unseemly. If he hadn't been so hungry for her she'd have died of mortification.

Clearing her throat she broached her next question, thankful yet again for this unconditional friendship.

"So, um, hygiene wise, what are the rules of contact after one or the other has had their mouth on the other's genitals?"

This time Sophie didn't try and cover her laughter, and Sara hoped like hell that Robert was far, far away from the conversation.

"Isn't genitals a bit like 'flaccid' and 'penis'? I think we should definitely ban that one too," she spluttered. "You mean after you've gone down on each other, should you then kiss?" Sophie softened her voice, obviously realizing that although there was an element of humour to the conversation, Sara was invested in the answer.

"It's all a matter of what you're comfortable with honey. There's no right or wrong way to have sex, so long as you're both enjoying it. And using contraception. Use a condom at all times, and double-up by being on the pill. Trust me."

Sara grinned, picturing an eight-month pregnant Sophie. While she was sad that, because of the distance, she hadn't seen Sophie since her accidental pregnancy, she was looking forward to flying out to the country to visit with her once the baby was born. And she knew absolutely that Sophie had no regrets about the way her life had changed since she'd met Robert and moved to live with him on his farm.

"Speaking of genitals, you'll never guess what my high and mighty Editor is making me write about now," she grumbled.

"I've missed your Bridgette stories, what's the witch doing now?"

"It's my own fault, I was telling her about an absurd trend in the US just as a laugh, and now she's determined we stay ahead of the curve and report about it here. But I feel like that's perpetuating the ridiculousness of it and I don't want to be held responsible for Australian women taking up the fad."

"What fad? I'm intrigued now."

"Whitening cream."

"Whitening cream isn't a new trend."

"It is when it's used on your butt."

"What?!"

"Apparently it's the latest craze in California," confirmed Sara dryly.

"Wow, so having a white butt hole is the next big thing. Who knew?"

"Aren't you glad your best friend is in the beauty industry and keeping you up to date on all these important developments?"

They both burst into laughter.

"Oh stop. Stop! I'm going to pee myself!" cried Sophie.

"Look, I've got to go, I told Robert I'd bring some morning tea out to him on the tractor. But call me anytime if you need to know *anything*. I mean it. And I also expect a phone call from you *as soon* as you do the deed. Like, send me a sneaky text when he gets up to dispose of the condom. Promise?"

"Promise."

Later that afternoon Sara was absorbed in writing her profile on Mitch. Even setting aside the charisma and sex appeal, he was an incredibly interesting interview subject.

He was business savvy and witty, and peppered his conversations with amusing anecdotes that Sara knew her readers would love. Remembering his request to 'take it easy on him', she paused in her typing. He clearly had demons he didn't want to share with her, and she wondered if they'd get to the point where he'd trust her enough to share all of his past. Regardless, she couldn't help admiring him for how far he'd come. His breathtaking apartment above PACIFIC was something even her parents would approve of.

The thought of her parents meeting Mitch had her fingers stilling on the keyboard again. While she'd had reservations about hooking up with Mitch because he was so far removed from her world, she'd not contemplated them ever actually *meeting*. So why was she now?

Mitch was an experience. An amazing, incredible, *earthshattering* experience. But one that would eventually be put behind her as they both moved on with their respective lives. He was a memory she'd discuss with Sophie from time to time, a delicious knowledge she'd relive in the privacy of her thoughts.

Because while she saw past the wild urban exterior of Mitch to the quality of man beyond his rough upbringing and beneath his tattoo-covered skin, she doubted her parents ever would.

Sara saw the depth of Mitch's bond with his family, the care and respect he afforded his employees, the determination and strength that had built him up from the gutters of his childhood.

But as much as she loved her mother and father, they would never look to see the real Mitch. And if she were honest with herself, if it hadn't been for the undeniable sexual attraction, Sara would never have looked either.

Pushing away from the desk and walking into the kitchen to dispose of the coffee mug on the sink, she thought it was just as well they weren't aware of her current hiatus from husband hunting.

As though on cue, her phone rang.

"Hi Mum."

"Sara honey, I just wanted to thank you for stepping up yesterday and joining the committee, I really do appreciate it."

"I know, it's okay. It was actually kind of fun. I had no idea of the logistics that go into an event – you women could capably manage the entire country, and still have time to play bridge."

Sara loved the sound of her mother's laugh. She had a social laugh, which was high and slightly brittle, but the laugh she reserved for her daughter was genuine, filled with all those tiny moments of shared warmth between them.

"Well, it was nice to have an injection of youth into the proceedings. And it didn't hurt that you met Amanda Cartwright, you know both her sons are in banking in

Melbourne. I wonder if they're coming back for the benefit?" she mused, half to herself.

"*Please* don't use this event as a match-making exercise. Please."

"I'm not!" her mother was indignant. "I was just thinking out loud. Besides, you're obviously bringing Phil to the dinner."

"Actually," she paused, taking a breath. "I'm not."

"You're what?"

"I'm not bringing Phil. We were never serious, and we're not seeing each other anymore."

The relief from that announcement was stunning. All of a sudden her lungs could expand to their full capacity and the rush of oxygen was liberating.

"Well. Well," her mother huffed. "I can't imagine what Darla thinks of this. Really Sara, Phil was such a catch!"

"Just not the catch for me."

"So, you're not coming with a date?"

"Yes. No. I mean yes, I am bringing a date. It's someone new, no one you'd know," she tacked on the end before her mother could question his pedigree.

Up until now Sara hadn't entertained the idea of taking Mitch, and even now she wasn't sure if she'd be brave enough to ask him. If she was brave enough to take him. But the thought sent a thrill of anticipation fluttering in her stomach.

"Well if he's no one I'd know, then I'm not sure he's someone you need to know sweetheart. Your father and I have connections, and you'd be wise to use them young lady."

"Mum!" Half-heartedly, Sara protested. She knew her objections fell on deaf ears. And really, until she decided to actually ask Mitch, and he said yes, it wasn't worth having this discussion.

"Okay honey, stop fretting. I'm just trying to help. You know I was – "

"Married by my age," Sara finished. "I know, I know. I'm got to go Mum, I'm trying to finish some work. I'll talk to you soon, Okay? Love you."

"Love you too honey."

Putting her phone down deliberately gently, Sara closed her eyes. Sometime over the last couple of weeks the idea of getting married had lost all its allure. All of a sudden she was questioning the trajectory of her life and doubting her parents focus. It was unnerving.

Ignoring the temptation of a walk along the coastline, she returned to the desk in the little window nook in her bedroom, determined to finish this first draft of the profile.

She'd then give herself a day away from it before editing, and handing it over to the sub editor. She preferred her work as polished as possible before Bridgette ever set eyes on the 'first' draft.

Settling onto her chair in a cross-legged position her phone beeped with an incoming text message.

Mitch: Thinking about me?
Sara: Hard not to. I'm writing your profile.
Mitch: All good things, of course.
Sara: Mostly.

Catching sight of her reflection in the mirror above her dressing table, Sara rolled her eyes. She was grinning like a lunatic. Mitch had a way of making her feel like a lovesick teenager and she wasn't sure if she liked that or not.

Mitch: You said soon.

Sara: Soon?

Mitch: You'd see me soon. Is it soon yet?

Sara: You don't want me to rush this masterpiece, do you?

Mitch: I want you to rush over here.

Sara: Tonight?

Mitch: Yes.

Sara grinned wider.

Sara: I'll bring Thai. Any requests?

Mitch: Naked.

Sara: Naked Thai?

Mitch: Naked you.

Sara: That can probably be arranged.

Several hours later Sara discarded her third outfit choice, letting it pool unheeded around her feet as she flipped through her wardrobe yet again, clothes hangers clattering against each other in her mounting frustration.

Cool, calm and collected Sara had left the building, and in her place stood a frenzied madwoman who couldn't for the life of her decide what to wear.

Sara had impeccable taste when it came to fashion. It helped that her budget wasn't exactly limited and she could supplement from the fashion editors at work. So the fact she now couldn't find something was, frankly, unacceptable.

Slumping onto her bed she eyed her wardrobe with irritation. Ever since she'd met Mitch it seemed her emotions were on hyper drive – from extreme dislike to excessive lust.

"Well what the hell *should* I wear to lose my virginity in?" she muttered, throwing a pair of jeans off the bed. She contemplated calling Sophie again, but knew Sophie's only concern would be lingerie, and Sara had that covered. It was what to wear *over* the black silk panties and demi-cup bra that was eluding her.

She wanted to keep it casual, but still look like she'd made an effort. Just not too *much* of an effort. And practical. She didn't want to trip over her own feet while wiggling out of clothes in the heat of the moment. Why had no one invented clothes that melted off when sexual energy reached a certain point?

Sighing, she kicked off the maxi skirt she had on and reached into her closet again…

———

Maggie was in a foul mood and it was providing a sufficient enough distraction for Mitch, who was pretending he wasn't obsessively counting down the minutes until Sara arrived.

His stomach was swooping and dipping and he momentarily panicked he was coming down with gastro, before recognizing it for the nerves it was.

Jesus Christ, could I stop acting like a teenager?

"Come on Mag, I know your ex is a total jerkwad but he has a right to see Ruby and you know he's got his mother there too. Everything will be fine," he leaned his hip against the kitchen bench, watching Maggie scrub viciously at the perfectly clean surface.

"I hate that he gets to have anything to do with her," she ceased her violent cleaning and swung to face Mitch. "And you know what I *really* hate?" she didn't give Mitch a chance to respond. "It *kills me* that she was so excited to see him, when I know he couldn't give a toss about seeing her, he's just doing it to mess with me."

Her shoulders, which had been so rigid with rage, rounded and slumped as the first tears started to roll down her face. "And now he's bloody making me cry again."

"I'm so sorry Maggie, about everything." He pulled her into him for a hug, wishing he could take away all the hurt. What he wouldn't give for five minutes alone with Maggie's ex in a dark alley. But he wasn't 17 anymore and knew he'd been damn lucky to walk away free the last time he'd faced Maggie's demons for her.

Maggie pulled back, roughly wiping her face with her hands. "Great, now I've just rubbed lemon-scented chemical all over my face," she groaned. "I'm going to have a shower and then get out of your hair, sitting in a dark movie cinema is just what I feel like. And I wouldn't want to be a third wheel on your *date*."

Her eyebrows raised in mischief on the last word. She had a little sister's curiosity about Sara and was enjoying teasing him about his "social climbing".

"I like her, don't get me wrong," she continued, "But she's *really* different to your usual hook up." Her eyes narrowed speculatively, waiting for his response.

"Don't call her a hook up, she's more than that," he muttered, shoving his hands through his hair. "She's... I don't know."

But he did know. He didn't want to slot her into the same

category as the often nameless, and quickly forgotten, women he'd slept with over the years. She meant more to him than that and, honestly, it scared the crap out of him.

"She's the kind of woman you could have forever with. But we both know I'm not the kind of man that's good with that kind of commitment. I failed mum, I wasn't there for you when you needed it. It sounds stupid to say it, but I'm not worthy of her."

Maggie was staring at him, her mouth agape.

"Are you kidding me right now?" she all but screeched. "I know I'm the little sister and usually my job is to bring you down a notch or two, but you're actually sounding kind of crazy right now. You're not worthy? That's the most fucked up thing I've ever heard." She stamped her foot for emphasis.

"Mum was an addict, and neither you nor I could have changed the way her story ended. And you *did* save me, we both know exactly what Leon would have done if you hadn't shown up when you did. You, big brother, need to grow the fuck up and stop letting the past fester. You're an amazing brother, Ruby thinks the sun literally shines out of your ass, and you've got a kick-ass career. So if I hear you say anything about being unworthy again, I'm going to seriously lose it."

She was breathless by the time she finished her rant, and Mitch was speechless.

"Well?" she demanded, raising an eyebrow at his muteness.

"Go and shower little sis, you stink," he said, grabbing at the discarded cleaning cloth and throwing it at her head.

Maggie had just left and Mitch was almost climbing out of his skin with anticipation, even though Sara wasn't due to arrive for another hour. Having already changed the sheets on his bed – accompanied by Maggie's annoying commentary – and put some red wine on the bench to breathe, he was drumming his fingers on his knees as he tried to relax on the sofa.

Thinking about the night ahead was getting him increasingly wound up. Maggie may have been off-course about his worthiness of being with Sara, but she was also right – Sara *was* different. Hell, she was the kind of girl who organized black tie charity dinners for Christ's sake. What the hell was she doing wasting time on him? Because he sure as hell wasn't husband material. At least not *her* kind of husband.

He laughed dryly, knowing that if he were to attend a black tie dinner he'd need to watch *Pretty Woman* beforehand, to get his cutlery etiquette correct. Even then he'd probably stuff up and embarrass her.

Slapping his hands down on his thighs he stared around the apartment. He needed to do something. Anything. Spying his laptop he jumped to his feet, Jennifer was going to fall over backwards when they had their weekly meeting on Monday and he'd actually read her notes for once.

Clicking through to his emails he chuckled at the subject of Jennifer's email: 'Monday's Agenda; not that you'll read this'. Hiring Jennifer had been a lucky fluke, but making her part-owner was one of the smartest things he'd done. It was her competency that was largely managing the studio while he worked on the financials and the future. He hadn't given a shit that she couldn't bring any money into the business, she was smart and loyal and an asset the business needed, especially with their plans to open a second studio within the next six months.

Remembering a comment from Simon, he made a mental note to ask Jennifer about her current boyfriend. Mitch hadn't yet met him, but apparently he was a douche. Simon had overheard a conversation when Jennifer had him on speaker phone, and his attitude bordered on disrespectful.

Mitch felt a big-brother protectiveness towards Jennifer and could feel his previous jittery anticipation morph to a mild anxiety. He of all people knew how many shitty people there were in this world, and what exactly they were capable of. He was going to organize an "accidental" meeting with this boyfriend as soon as possible.

True to character, he closed the laptop before opening Jennifer's email and stood, shaking his body like a big dog. He needed to loosen the hell up before Sara arrived.

Grabbing at his keys he jammed his feet into a pair of worn Converse and headed out, taking the stairs instead of the elevator in a bid to expend energy. Coming out the building's front door he breathed the salt air deep. God he loved living on the beach. The palm trees that lined the middle of the street twinkled with lights and the laidback vibe of Bondi never failed to charm him after the frenetic pace of LA.

Stretching out his long legs he strode to the gelato shop on the corner where, thanks to his sweet tooth, they knew him by name.

"What'll it be this evening?" greeted Jeff, the college student who worked here part-time. Jeff had visited Mitch's studio last month to get his first tattoo, and had since confided that the ladies liked it, very much.

Mitch viewed gelato much like he did women – he appreciated the flavors but didn't have a favourite. Eyes roaming over the frosted delights behind the glass counter, he wondered what Sara's flavor preference was. He suspected that with her ever-changing fragrance and eye colour, she didn't have a favourite either.

"I'll go a couple of small tubs tonight and cover all my bases," Mitch said. "Apple Pie, and that chocolate one with the peanut fudge. And the raspberry sorbet too. Thanks mate."

As Jeff scooped out the order his thoughts strayed to the notion of eating dessert off Sara's body. Positioned between her legs with his hands firmly holding her hips as his head bent and licked at the melting gelato on her stomach, dipping and swirling his tongue into the hollow of her bellybutton, sucking on the smoothness of her bare skin…

"That's thirty dollars thanks."

Mitch jerked out of his daydream and hastily pulled money from his wallet. Blood had pumped to his cock making it throb, and Mitch was thankful his shirt covered the evidence of his arousal. This Pavlovian response to Sara was getting out of hand. He couldn't help but wonder if it would be easier, or harder, after he slept with her.

CHAPTER 11

If Sara wasn't worried about the takeaway Thai getting even colder in its containers, she'd have walked another lap around the block. Nerves were warring with her anticipation and she wasn't sure which was going to win.

Stopping for the second time in front of the glass door of Mitch's apartment building, she eyed her reflection critically. Her bedroom floor was currently littered with the contents of her wardrobe, but she was happy with the simple wrap dress she'd eventually settled on. A dress seemed the appropriate easy-access outfit to lose your virginity in.

A fine, rose gold chain necklace was her only accessory and, for once, she kept her makeup minimal; primer with a mineral powder foundation, a single coat of mascara and a slick of her favourite sheer lip gloss.

There was no point in hiding behind makeup when the man was going to be seeing her naked. And she didn't care how long-lasting her makeup might claim to be – she was pretty damn sure it was going to look a sweaty mess by the time she was finished tonight.

The main reason she was wanting to hightail it home – Thai or no Thai – was that she hadn't put in coloured contacts. They'd become almost a form of armour for her, much the same as makeup. And for the first time ever, Mitch would be seeing her real eye colour. She had no idea why this seemed so momentous. It's not like she'd forgone contacts altogether and wore her glasses. And he probably wouldn't notice anyway.

Giving herself a mental slap, Sara watched her reflection straighten her shoulders and shake her hair back. It was game time. She was walking in here and eating this damn Thai and then losing her virginity.

Resolved, she marched herself indoors to the lift and pushed the button to Mitch's floor. The door opened straight away, not allowing her momentum to be slowed so that she arrived at Mitch's door short of breath, as though she'd taken the stairs instead of the lift. Pausing, she attempted to compose herself.

This was happening. She was about to lose her virginity. Finally. And it was going to be with a *ridiculously* sexy man. Hell yes this was happening.

Raising a steady hand she knocked quickly, deliberately.

The door swung open and Mitch's bulk filled the doorframe. After hours of wanting, he was *so close* and Sara's pupils dilated as she took him in. He was all male and *all* delicious. Screw the Thai, Sara was ready to feast on him.

His eyes were just as devouring as he silently drew her inside and crowded her against the closed door. Without breaking eye contact he took the takeout food bag, dropping it to the floor. His big hand palmed her cheek as he tilted her face further upwards.

"They're grey. Your eyes are grey," he muttered. "Are they your real colour?"

She nodded, nerves and excitement rendering her mute.

"Like smooth stones at the bottom of a clear pond."

She didn't have time to process the surprisingly poetic description before both his hands cupped her face and he kissed her gently, sweetly, but with a banked heat that promised so much more.

She gave herself up to the mastery of his mouth as his lips slanted over hers and his tongue demanded entry. Neither closed their eyes, watching each other as they breathed shared air.

He pulled back and she blinked. It was just a simple kiss and her mind was already scrambled.

"I really like the grey. They're beautiful," he said. "You shouldn't cover them with coloured lenses."

Consumed as she was by his proximity – by the breadth of his shoulders above her and that essential male, husky scent of his – Sara could only blink again.

Even if she wanted to, there was no chance her brain was functioning at a level that would allow her to form the necessary words to explain she was currently wearing normal, clear contacts. Why were they even talking about her eyes?

All she wanted right now, all she *needed* right now, was to fall into their sexual chemistry. To sink into it, and drown. It was way past the time to speak, or think. It was time to *do*.

"I think we should forget dinner and skip straight to the naked part," she murmured, stretching onto tiptoes so she could reach around his neck and draw him down for another drugging kiss.

Sara had kissed men before. Hell, as someone who didn't go much further than kissing, she had become well versed in the art of first base. But holy hell if Mitch didn't make caressing lips transcend the actual act.

His seeking, plundering tongue had her head spinning and the careful way his hand cupped the back of her head made her toes curl in feminine delight.

If Sara could climb into his skin right now, she would. With panting breath her eager hands delved beneath his shirt to reach the smooth skin of his bunched abdominal muscles, tantalizingly ripped.

Her hands skated upwards, brushing the pads of her thumbs over his nipples and he groaned, catching her bottom lip in a bite. Sucking it in apology, he moved down her throat, lips whisper light and beard stubble deliciously scratching. The touch of his tongue soothed the frantic flutter of her pulse, licking that sensitive hollow at the base of her throat.

She shuddered a sigh, acknowledging in a far-off part of her brain that being weak at the knees was more than just an expression. She was about to melt into a puddle at his feet. And wasn't *that* an interesting thought. Because she was sure there were some very interesting things she could do to him from that position.

"Bed. Now," he demanded, stepping back and catching her hand as it fell displaced from within his shirt. He brought her inner wrist to his lips and inhaled, closing his eyes. "You have no idea the effect you have on me Princess."

"Oh I think I do," she grinned, quirking an eyebrow and glancing at the impressive erection evident at the front of his jeans.

His eyes turned serious.

"And you're sure you're ready?"

"Beyond ready," she assured him.

"Because we're going to take this slow, okay? And we can stop anytime you feel uncomfortable."

"Can we hurry up and get to the bedroom so we can start the slow part?"

His voice dropped low and dirty.

"My pleasure."

Bedside table lamps threw the room into pleasantly dim relief, allowing mood lighting that hinted at a remove from everyday life. It was just the two of them, caught together in this moment in time, exploring the possibility between them.

True to his word there was nothing hurried about Mitch as he stood over her reclining form on the bed and shucked his shirt, revealing a study in perfection. The sculpted muscles of his torso were highlighted by tattoos, and a smattering of hair led in a tantalizing trail beneath the waistband of his jeans.

Mesmerized, Sara could feel her thumping heartbeat echoing in the throb between her legs and she caught herself before she licked her lips.

"You could model you know," she mused, propping herself up on bent elbows. "I'm sure there's a whole sub-culture of women out there who totally dig the Viking warrior look."

He smirked and popped the top button of his jeans, easing the denim down thick thighs and long legs to pool at his feet.

She bit her bottom lip in an effort to restrain a moan of appreciation. He was sans underwear, and his cock rose proud and free. And *holy hell* did it rise. Mitch casually dragged a hand up the length and Sara couldn't have looked away if she tried. And she was *not* trying.

She sucked in a lungful of air, and then a second for good measure. She was so enraptured with objectifying Mitch that she was in danger of asphyxiation.

The man was a glory of masculine precision – every tendon and sinew, muscle and ligament in perfect alignment. His bicep flexed as his hand did another sweep of his cock, his thighs spread and his abdomen reflexively clenching.

In one smooth move he was on the bed between her legs, his hands rucking her dress around her hips as his mouth pressed hotly against her stomach. "I don't need a sub-culture of women. I just need you."

Sliding her panties off he dipped his head between her legs, urging her leg over his shoulder as he wedged himself between her spread thighs with a sigh of contentment. Sara tensed, her hands gripping at the mattress beneath her. She hadn't expected the shock of intimacy such an act would have and, as much as she craved his touch, she couldn't fight the urge to clamp her legs together.

Mitch didn't move – not that he could with her vice-like grip – except to rub his hands rhythmically up the outside of her thighs, soothing and reassuring. She relaxed her hold marginally.

"It's okay Sara, I promise you'll like it," he assured, voice muffled.

She relaxed further.

She had no doubt she was going to like it, hell, she planned on *loving* it. It was just that a man had his head buried between her legs, and it was a little disconcerting.

When he started mouthing hot air on her labia, hands on the insides of her thighs edging them wider still, she relaxed further. Oh yeah, she could probably get used to this. The stroke of his tongue made her jump and when he expertly found her clit she found her hands tangled in his hair, urging him on.

That tongue of his was circling and flicking and about to drive her crazy. Inserting first one finger, and then two, he mimicked the circling of his tongue, alternating with slow deep pumps that increased in pressure and pace until the intensity was almost beyond bearing.

Sara was mindless and wanton. Her world had shrunk to Mitch, and the incredible things his mouth was doing to her. Flares of pleasure were popping behind closed eyelids and the trembling intensity of her orgasm built and built, before cresting and crashing through her, causing her to thrash her head and cry out before falling limp against the mattress.

She could feel him rising, moving up her body and coming to rest beside her. She cracked open an eyelid and saw him wiping the back of his hand across his mouth, which glistened with her wetness. And holy shit was that a turn on.

"That was amazing," he sighed, his eyes roving over her spent body.

"You stole my line. I'm pretty sure that's what I'm meant to say," she replied, closing her eye again. "But you've done yourself a disservice. I don't think I need to have sex after having experienced that. I'm happy now. I could die right now, and not have a single regret."

"Oh Princess, you don't know the half of it yet."

———

Mitch's body heat was jacked way up, and he didn't think he'd ever been this turned on in his life. He didn't know he'd been starving until he'd tasted her. She was everything he didn't know he wanted, and he knew beyond any doubt that this woman would leave an indelible mark on him.

Adrenaline coursed through him, tempered by a hum of satisfaction. He was the reason Sara lay flushed and sated before him, and damn if it didn't make him feel like a conquering hero.

"Time to get out of the rest of your clothes Princess," he said, helping her to sit and remove her dress and bra.

Running a fingertip over the crest of her breast he couldn't quite believe he was going to be the first man to have her like this. The urge to claim her was roaring inside him, even as his mind cautioned restraint and an unhurried, deliberate approach.

He was going to take this slow for her, even if it killed him.

Those pouty lips of hers opened on a gasp as his mouth closed around her nipple, sucking it to a peaked tip and then laving it with his tongue as he palmed the other breast, weighty and firm.

Moving over her, he pushed her back against the mattress and alternated between her breasts, lavishing attention as her breathing grew erratic and choppy, her body starting to hum again as he ran his hands all over it.

"Okay, so maybe I do need sex after all," she breathed, wrapping a leg around his waist to lock him closer. Fingers that were twisting in his hair tugged his head up to her lips, which he met readily. Without breaking contact he moved up her body until he held himself over her, supported by his elbows.

Losing himself in their kiss he forgot everything but the taste of her mouth, the sound of her moaning, the feel of her moving restlessly beneath him. It wasn't until her hand wrapped around his cock that the trance was broken, and not before his hips reflexively pumped in need.

Raising his head he looked down on her, at the colour

riding high on her cheeks and her bed ravaged hair. Her eyelids drifted closed and her lips parted on a sigh as her hand rubbed the length of his cock, her other hand drifting to lightly cup his balls.

"Babe, you've got to stop," he choked out, rolling to his side and out of reach of her questing hands.

Her eyes sprang open and her hands fell against her stomach.

"Stop?" the question was unsure. "I thought – "

"I'm not stopping, *you're* stopping," he clarified. "There's no way in hell I can do this the right way if you touch me."

"The right way?" she rolled onto her side to bring their bodies flush, her breasts pressing against his chest and her legs tangling between his.

"Hand on heart this is going to be good for you Sara. But you've got to let me do it my way."

He'd promised to worship her body, and he had no plans to renege on that. He could spend forever touching her, kissing her, adoring every inch of her. But the moment she touched his cock he couldn't guarantee he wouldn't lose all sense of reason. The last thing he wanted was to rush this.

Her first time was going to be as perfect as he could make it.

"I get it, we're going slow," she complained, breathing into his neck and then nipping with her teeth. "But I don't have to like it."

"You're going to like it alright," he said, pushing her over onto her back again and settling between the nirvana of her spread thighs.

Christ this just might kill him.

Bending his head he feathered whisper light kisses along

her neck, reveling in the knowledge he was driving her crazy as her head tipped back in abandon. Tonguing along her clavicle his hand roamed down, slipping between her legs where she unashamedly rocked into his palm.

"Okay, I like it. More." She demanded on a pant, her hands clenching the bed sheets. "Jesus Mitch, more!"

He chuckled and slipped a finger inside her, groaning at the feel of her tight slickness. He inserted another and started a slow, rhythmic thrusting, which her hips mirrored in perfect synchronization.

"Open your eyes baby, I want you watching me as I take you over the edge again," he said, adding his circling thumb to her clit.

"Oh!" her hips bucked and pressed closer to him as he picked up the pace and sent her soaring, her orgasm shuddering through them both.

He slowed his fingers but didn't remove them, while his other hand was squeezing, kneading, stroking any part of her body he could reach.

The desire in her eyes was a tangible thing and, with her eyes still locked on his, she lifted her hips in tacit permission, her need entreating him.

Disengaging momentarily he reached into the bedside drawer for a condom and sheathed himself. With his heart in his throat he lowered his body fully atop hers and she took his weight with a throaty sigh.

The strain of holding back had his forearms trembling and his shoulders bunching tightly. Concentrating fiercely on every nuance of her expression he positioned the head of his cock at her entrance.

He was desperate with desire that was tinged with fear.

The responsibility of what he was about to do weighed heavily. But *Jesus Christ* she was undulating beneath him, her softness contrasting with his hardness, her arms were wrapped around him and her fingers were digging into his back. He wanted her more than he wanted his next breath. In fact, oxygen was highly over-rated.

"Mitch," she pleaded, her eyes bright and beseeching. "I need this. I need you."

He lowered his head to take her lips once again – open mouthed, raw and unrestrained. Distracting her with the kiss, he flexed his hips and guided his cock into her, slowly but surely. As he breached her entrance she gasped, tensing, and he stilled instantly.

"Baby are you okay?" He was surprised he could force words out.

"It's okay. It's just – a lot. Don't stop."

Resting his forehead against hers, watching her wide eyes, he pushed against the slight resistance until he was all in.

"Oh fuck," he moaned involuntarily, closing his eyes. He opened them as her chest heaved on a deep breath, her body relaxing into the mattress.

"Okay, that's – good," she said on a shaky sigh.

"Good?"

"It stung. And I feel, stretched. But not in a bad way."

He made to ease back out and she wrapped her legs around him, holding him to her. "No, don't pull out, just give me a minute."

Blood was loud, pounding through his ears and Mitch was surprised the tension in him wasn't vibrating them both. He'd never been this tightly wound in his life.

Sara relaxed further and gave an experimental rock of her

hips. He clenched his buttocks and willed his body to remain rock solid still, ignoring the instinctual need to thrust. To claim.

He'd never felt such a deep connection to his base masculinity as he did at this moment and the depth of this intimacy with Sara was shocking.

She gave a tentative smile. "You look like you're the one in pain."

"Are you in pain?" he was sure panic flashed across his face.

"No, I'm fine. But you need to relax."

"Babe, I'm balls deep and trying to be gentle. It's a bit hard to relax."

"Just let's take it slow, okay?"

His grin was slightly feral and to hide his base need he kissed her, plundering her with his tongue that he matched with gentle thrusts of his hips – a slow back and forth that built the inferno hungering inside.

His lips moved to the side of her neck, sucking and kissing as he caressed her breast, fingers plucking at her nipple and making her moan. Because concentrating on her, on her every small reaction, was the only way he was going to starve off his own orgasm that was hammering for release.

Clenching his jaw he continued his steady rocking movement and was rewarded with Sara's breathy moans, her nails digging into his back, her pelvis tilting to allow deeper penetration.

Lifting his torso further he reached between them, her gasp turning to a moan as his thumb sought her sensitive nub. He bit down on her shoulder as his cock continued its tender assault and she squirmed in pleasure.

"Mitch! It's too much. It's –" she swallowed back another moan.

"Do you want me to stop?"

"Don't you dare!"

He moaned himself. She felt so fucking good.

"Babe I can't hold out much longer."

"Faster Mitch. Harder."

Increasing the tempo, his thumb strumming her clit as their sweat-slicked bodies slapped against each other until her whole body went taunt and she cried out her climax, shuddering against him.

It was too much for Mitch, who thrust again once, twice and then went over the edge himself, clutching Sara to him while his orgasm racked his body as all his tactile senses rushed together. Groaning into her shoulder in relief he held tight, not sure if the release of pressure might be akin to dying. A really fucking pleasurable death.

The intensity of sharing this intimacy was almost beyond comprehension. It was so far beyond sex that Mitch was reeling, even as his heart rate dropped back to normal and his breathing evened out.

Hand on heart I am in way too deep with this woman.

CHAPTER 12

Lying in Mitch's arms, Sara was aware of every inch of her body. She felt lit up from the inside out and was half surprised she wasn't glowing. Post-orgasm euphoria made her heavy and languorous, but also hypersensitive to every touch.

She had a stinging soreness between her legs now that he'd withdrawn, but it was almost pleasurable in a strange way.

The satisfaction he'd wrought from her went a long way to dulling the discomfit.

The concept of losing her virginity felt overshadowed by the act itself, which was less about it being the first time and more about it being the first time with *Mitch*. Now that they'd had sex, the idea of losing her virginity seemed less momentous and more inevitable.

Mitch's hands hadn't ceased roaming over her bare skin, sweeping the length of her back and curving up her side to palm a breast. His constant contact saved Sara from feeling awkward now that the rush of lust had been fulfilled.

It felt right to be lying naked with this man.

Cupping her bottom he shifted her up, so their faces rested on the pillow next to each other. His finger traced lightly over her face, his own creasing into a smile.

"How do you feel?"

She took a moment to consider.

"I'm okay. It was good."

He raised an eyebrow.

"Well that's a boost for my ego."

She fought back a grin.

"It might have been better than good. Like kind of amazing," she admitted.

"But are you sore?"

Sara felt a rush of warmth at his concern. Who knew the Viking warrior could be so considerate?

"A little."

"I should say I'm sorry, but I'm not," and he claimed her lips in a leisurely, decadent kiss.

"In fact, this has been the best bad decision I've ever made."

"So I'm a bad decision?" She pretended outrage, nipping at his neck with sharp teeth. "If anything, *you're* the bad decision."

"Yes Princess, I absolutely am. You couldn't have chosen someone more wrong for you."

"And yet you turned out to be so *right*," she sighed into his mouth, rubbing her swollen lips over his.

Her stomach growled and he pulled back, laughing.

"Hungry are you Princess?"

Her stomach growled again.

"The takeaway is probably stone cold by now," she pouted. "I'm going to starve to death."

He dropped a kiss on her forehead as he rolled off the bed and onto his feet, fiercely beautiful and confident in his nudity.

"So dramatic, Princess. I'll heat the food up and bring it back and we can eat in bed."

Sara stared after his delectable ass as he walked out of the room, and then fell back onto the pillow. She was deliriously content and didn't want to leave his bed, ever, but the thought struck her that she should use the bathroom. Hadn't she read somewhere you should pee after sex to avoid getting a urinary tract infection?

Urgh. How completely un-sexy to be thinking about a UTI after the most amazing sexual experience of my life.

Scrambling from the bed, she shrugged into Mitch's discarded shirt and entered the ensuite bathroom where she quickly relieved herself and used a washcloth to clean between her legs – where she was definitely feeling the effects of her newly de-virginised state.

Ready for damage control she faced her reflection in the mirror, only to pause in surprise. She'd been expecting wildly mussed hair and raccoon mascara streaks, but instead she was bright eyed and glowing, with tousled hair that usually only came from paying big bucks at a hair salon.

So this is what they call a post coital glow.

Slipping back into bed she picked up her phone to text Sophie.

Sara: Sex is amazing.

Sophie: !!!!!!!! Can you hear me squealing? I'm so happy for you.

Sara: Call you in the morning.

Sophie: You better. I want ALL the details.

The deliciously distinctive aroma of Thai preceded Mitch as he returned, having already dished the food into large ceramic bowls. Handing one to Sara he set his own down and took the bottle of wine from beneath his arm, pouring generous glasses before settling onto the bed beside her.

"Are you blushing?" he asked, taking a large mouthful and watching her with laughing eyes.

"No!" She dipped her eyes. "Okay, maybe."

"I think we're past embarrassment, aren't we?"

"I'm not embarrassed. It's just, *you're* not embarrassed and you're very naked."

"And you're very not. As hot as you look wearing my clothes, it's much more fun being naked."

"But we're *eating*."

"I know, and next is dessert. Which I'm going to eat off you."

Sara's appetite was all of a sudden replaced with a much more carnal one. Her discomfit at Mitch's nudity swiftly morphing into hot anticipation.

"Eat your food Princess, I don't want to have to heat it up a second time."

Captivated in a sudden haze of lust, she watched his throat as he took a sip of wine, and licked her own lips as he licked his. He was just so damn *virile*. Even though she was sore she yearned to feel the weight of his body again, to feel his cock inside her.

His hand cupping her cheek jolted out of her daze and she took a long swallow of her wine, attempting to hide her sudden lapse of reality.

"Babe, I really do need you to eat something. You're hungry, remember?"

"I think you've made me addicted to sex," she accused, setting her wine glass down on the bedside table and jabbing her fork in his direction. "I love eating, and I'm hungry. But all I can think about is your body!"

He smirked and said nothing, just leant over and took a prawn from her bowl of food and popped it in his mouth.

"I'm serious Mitch, I think you should put some clothes on. I can't concentrate."

"How about I distract you?"

"You *are* distracting me, that's the problem!"

"You eat, and I'll talk. Okay?"

Scooping some noodles into her mouth, Sara nodded. She really *was* hungry.

"Are you going to tell me all your dark and dirty secrets?"

"You wanted to know about my tattoos, I'll tell you about them."

"I think my looking at your tattoos is defeating the purpose of counter-distraction," she mumbled through another mouthful of noodles.

He laughed and pulled her toward him, his big hand cupping the back of neck and his lips brushing hers.

"You're adorable, you know that?"

They spent the next hour finishing the bottle of wine with Sara happily exploring every inch of his inked skin. She was intrigued by the way his tattoos were truly a history of his life, with an American eagle courtesy of his time in the US, and a Mexican sugar skull from a holiday in Cabo San Lucas. A tribal Maori sleeve from when he trained with a legendary tattoo artist in New Zealand and a magnificent lion head on his chest symbolizing his zodiac sign – even a small Japanese anime character from a stint in Japan. Scriptwork proclaimed 'every saint has a past and every sinner has a future' and an avenging angel dominated his back with intricate, sweeping wings dipping over his collarbones and onto his chest.

It was testament to the skill of the various tattoo artists who had worked on his skin that the whole effect was cohesive – a visual tapestry that bled seamlessly into each new element.

Sara's favourite was a sultry Vargas-style pinup girl gracing his left arm – there was something about the playfulness and sexuality the tattoo exuded that captured her interest. Her attention returned to it time and again.

"And her, the bombshell?" she finally asked, scraping her fingernail softly over the tattoo. "Does she represent an ex-girlfriend?"

There was a note in her voice that was off, and she cleared her throat. *Obviously* she didn't care about Mitch's past relationships, but it was kind of weird to be in such an intimate situation with him and think of his sexual past.

What kind of woman would engender such passion in her man that he'd forever mark himself in her honour?

"Ah Vivian," he said fondly, "She's pretty special."

Who the fuck is Vivian and what made her *so special?*

Sara's back teeth ground together as she attempted to keep her tone light.

"Vivian was your girlfriend?"

"No, I just thought she looked like a Vivian. Sal, one of the artists I worked with in LA, had built her reputation on tattooing pinup girls – her Grandfather was a US serviceman who served in World War II. He met Sailor Jerry while stationed in Hawaii and it was his tattoos that sparked Sal's passion."

"Sailor Jerry the ginger rum?"

"Sailor Jerry the tattoo artist legend; he was a sailor who mustered out of the Navy and settled in Honolulu, where he built his legacy. It's said that when he was first starting out in Chicago, he paid homeless men with cheap wine to practice on them. And now he's known as the father of old-school tattoo design."

Sara *desperately* wanted to know if Sal was the girlfriend, or if the tattoo was simply in homage to the artist's particular skill and an industry icon.

Her fingers twitched, she wanted to ask so bad.

But whatever it was they were doing, it wasn't serious, and she absolutely did *not* need to know the answer.

"You want to know if Sal was my girlfriend," Mitch stated with unnerving perception.

"Maybe. Okay, yes." No point being coy about it.

"She was just a friend. A really good friend. But she had mental health problems and I just, I didn't realise how serious it was until it was too late."

"Too late?"

"She took her own life. I was meant to meet her for lunch the day she did it, but I cancelled because I took a last-minute booking," he said shakily. "And I never saw her again."

"Oh God, I'm so sorry." Her heart squeezed in sympathy. "You know it wasn't your fault, right?"

His smile was tight and it didn't reach his eyes. "It might not have been my fault, but I sure as fuck didn't save her." He scrubbed a hand over his face. "I don't know, it probably explains my avoidance of commitment when it comes to relationships. I feel like I've failed a lot of the women in my life."

She started to say that it wasn't his job to save everyone, but he interrupted.

"What about you Princess, had any more thoughts on what we're tattooing on this silky skin of yours?" his stroking fingers distracted her, and the shivery heat that had been steadily building, sparked.

Breath hitching, all thoughts fled as he leaned closer and kissed the side of her neck, his tongue licking and teasing.

His lips moved to that sensitive spot behind her ear and she gasped. She felt his lips curve into a smile before he resumed his sensuous assault.

"You know what babe? We've got a lot of all night left, and I'm ready for dessert."

——

As Mitch grabbed the tubs of gelato from the freezer he clocked the time and grimaced – Maggie would be home from the cinema soon. While he'd thought he was long past the roommate phase of his life, he'd never once resented sharing his space with his sister and niece. But he'd also never brought a woman home.

He'd really prefer to ravish Sara without the threat of his sister overhearing them. Hopefully Maggie would have enough sense to go straight to her room and listen to music. Loudly.

"So my grey-eyed girl, I've got three flavours to choose from," he announced, setting the tubs on the bedside table. "But before you get to taste, you have to tell me why you wear coloured contacts."

Sara was deliciously naked and lounging against the pillows.

"How about I taste and tell?" she bargained, grabbing the spoon from him.

He grinned. He liked everything about this girl.

"Sure babe. Apple pie?"

"No way. Why ruin perfectly good ice-cream by adding fruit? What else do you have?"

"Chocolate with peanut fudge?"

"*Now* you're talking my language."

Watching her spoon ice-cream into her pretty mouth had his cock semi-hard in seconds. And when she moaned in appreciation? He was a goner.

"Good?"

"So good."

He couldn't wait any longer to taste that ice-cream on her lips. Leaning forward he pressed his mouth to hers, licking and sucking until she opened for him. The sweet taste of chocolate and fudge and *her* had him desperate.

But that fantasy of eating dessert from her body had him pulling back, even as she protested – wrapping her arms to link behind his neck, spoon dangling from her fingers.

"Mmmmmm. More please."

"No more for you, until you tell me about the contacts."

He had a theory that she was using the coloured contacts and the makeup – never overdone but always impeccable – as a form of armour, protecting herself against judgement. He was well aware that as a beauty writer she was expected to present herself a certain way, but he also wondered if it was a way of hiding – conforming to what was expected of her. And he suspected the majority of those expectations came from her parents.

She pouted her lips in a faux frown and it took everything in him not to devour her there and then.

Taking the spoon from her he scooped up more ice-cream and fed it to her, ignoring the slight shake of his arm as he struggled to rein in his desire. When the tip of her tongue swiped ice-cream from the corner of his mouth he groaned in frustration.

"There's no story to tell," she informed him, taking back the spoon and helping herself to the tub. "I am wearing contacts tonight, they're just clear. I need to wear either contacts or glasses, and I only ever wear glasses at home."

"Oh you are *so* going to wear those glasses for me," he promised. "I bet you look sexy as fuck in them."

"Don't tell me you have a librarian or secretary fetish?" she laughed.

"I have a Sara fetish," he growled, tugging her legs so that she slipped from the pillows and was flat on her back before him. "And now it's my turn."

She giggled, passing him the spoon and placing her hands behind her head so she could watch as he spooned the softening raspberry sorbet and dribbled it deliberately, slowly, onto her bare and quivering stomach.

She squealed at the icy contact, which soon turned to a breathy moan as the warmth of his lips met her skin. She was silky smooth and the sweet tartness of the sorbet had his tongue licking and lapping, chasing the small rivulets that slid down her side.

Sara's hips were undulating and, glancing up, he couldn't help comparing her to a reclining Greek goddess with her breasts heaving and her luxurious hair tumbling free.

She opened her eyes and caught his stare.

"Finished already?" That quirk of her eyebrow had his smirk re-emerging.

"Not even close Princess."

He could feast on her all. Night. Long.

Dropping down the bed he positioned himself between her legs, placing his palms on her inner thighs and pushing them further apart. He paused, taking in the glory that was her.

"You are so damn beautiful."

That flush was high on her cheeks again as she threw her head back in abandonment. Her confidence in her body, despite her lack of experience, was a huge turn on. As was her absolute trust in him as she shared this most intimate part of her.

He hadn't been exaggerating earlier when he'd promised their experience was going to be more than sex. He was ready to worship at her alter and for him, this was as close to a spiritual communion as he'd ever had. The intimacy he felt with her went beyond anything he'd ever known.

It didn't scare him, it goddamn terrified him.

But then she whimpered his name and he lost himself in her – in her taste, in her pleasure. Using his tongue, lips and teeth, he worked her over until she was panting and screaming, her thighs clenching and her hands twining ruthlessly into his hair.

It was his name on her lips as she tumbled into oblivion.

When her body slackened and her hands fell from his hair, he rose up on his haunches and looked his fill of her, reveling in her lushness. Loving that he could taste her in his mouth.

She opened one eye and grinned lazily.

"Nice work Viking."

"Just *nice*?"

She opened both eyes as he took his cock in hand, stroking its rigid length. He loved that she couldn't take her eyes off his slowly working fist.

"Come here Viking and let me reward you," she purred,

rising up on her elbows.

He wanted nothing more than to bury himself in her again, to wrap her legs around his hips and lose his ever loving mind.

But tonight was her first and she was undoubtedly tender – he was well aware his cock was larger than normal, twice in one night could elevate discomfort to pain. And there was no way he was risking that with her.

"Are you game Princess?" he asked instead, his fist continuing its leisurely action.

He saw curiosity flash in her grey eyes, even as her throat swallowed.

"I'm game," she breathed.

"Have you ever watched a man pleasure himself?"

Her eyes dropped once again to his straining cock and she answered without looking away.

"No."

"Do you want to?"

He could tell it was an illicit suggestion to her – her eyes widened and her breath audibly quickened.

"Yes."

"Touch yourself Sara. Touch your tits."

It was coarse language for a coarse instruction and his arousal spiked with her dilating pupils and mouth parting on a pant. His fist tightened as her hands rose to tentatively cup her breasts, their rosy pink nipples tightly ruched and begging to be sucked.

"Touch yourself how you want me to touch you. Imagine those are my hands," he instructed hoarsely.

Her eyes flashed to his before dropping again to encompass his clenching abdomen gleaming in a fine layer of sweat, his braced thighs and his hand – rhythmically pumping his cock.

He could feel it in his balls when those fingers of hers plucked at her nipples, pulling and rolling them between her thumbs.

"Does that feel good baby?"

Seemingly without thought, one of her hands drifted over her stomach and came to rest atop her spread thighs.

"Go on," he encouraged. "What would my hand do?"

Her eyes drifted shut as her index finger circled her clit and his control snapped. Frantically, harshly, he drove his fist up and down his cock, desperate for a release that had been building for far too long. The pressure was too much. The intensity caused a pounding of blood in his head that momentarily blocked out sound.

Bucking her hips, Sara cried out her orgasm and Mitch let his head fall back as he climaxed with unmitigated intensity, his ejaculation coating Sara's stomach.

Sound returning and heart beat slowing, he raised his head to find Sara's fingers lightly tracing through the cum on her skin and his cock throbbed in response.

He wondered how far he could push her.

"Put your fingers in your mouth Princess."

Her teeth snagged at her plump bottom lip, her softening nipples pebbled.

Even if she didn't do it, he knew the thought excited her.

Holding his breath, he watched as she raised her hand – opening her luscious mouth and sucking the fingers inside.

"*Fuuuuck*," he breathed out gutturally, falling onto the bed beside her and crushing her to his chest. "I don't think I'm ever going to get enough of you Princess."

CHAPTER 13

"It's good Sara, it's bloody good actually," commented Bridgett, continuing to scan Sara's first draft of Mitch's interview. "I like him. I think our readers will like him. When am I seeing photos to go with this?"

Working to tamp down the buzz from her boss's praise, Sara re-crossed her legs in the chair opposite. Pleasing her hard-nosed editor was no mean feat, and "bloody good" was akin to winning a Pulitzer Prize.

After the sexual awakening she'd had with Mitch last night, she was already walking on clouds. She was so glowy that three people had already asked what foundation she was wearing.

Shivering with remembered pleasure she had to force herself to concentrate.

"The shoot is set for this afternoon, in his tattoo studio. I've been over the brief with Kirsty and she thinks she can have proofs to us by Thursday at the latest."

"Good. You've proved yourself with this one Sara. I'd like to formally offer you Pauline's maternity leave position as deputy editor."

Oh. My. God.

"Thank you Bridgett, I'd love to take on the role."

Calm and composed. She doesn't need to know I'm about to pass out with excitement.

"Good. The HR department will be emailing you details."

Bridgett dropped the pages onto her desk and pushed her glasses to the top of her head. When Sara didn't immediately make a move to leave, she lifted her hand in a shooing gesture.

"Off you go then. Doesn't the Marketing Coordinator want to talk to you about some product placements?" Her tone was brusque and she was already tapping at her phone.

Summarily dismissed, Sara checked her own phone on the way out. Before watching her get into a taxi home last night, Mitch had promised to be in touch and, true to his word, he'd text this morning with a good morning beautiful message.

Humming under her breath, she came to a halt in front of her desk. She had *seven* missed calls from an unknown number, all in succession. And they hadn't left a voice message. Weird.

"I know, not your usual delivery, huh?"

Distracted, Sara looked up at her assistant, Becky, and saw the large white teddy bear – complete with red satin hearts on its paws – sitting before her. Despite its size, or perhaps because of, it looked cheap and unbearably tacky.

"Where did it come from?" she wondered as Becky came to stand beside her. Picking it up she could see there was no note or press release; "Which courier brought it? They'll know which PR it came from."

"That's the funny thing, he wasn't in a uniform and I'd never seen him before," said Becky, reaching for the bear and looking it over.

"Huh." Sara wasn't sure what else to say.

"It's so ugly it's almost cute," offered Becky, passing it back.

"Nope. Not even. It's just ugly."

"Maybe it's not from a PR and it's a secret admirer,"

Becky teased, waggling her eyebrows suggestively.

That gave Sara pause. Could Mitch have sent it? She wouldn't have thought stuffed toys were his style. And if he thought this was *her* style then she was kind of disappointed. She didn't want him to think he had to buy her anything, but if he was going to give her a gift then she wished he knew how juvenile this made him look and her feel.

Men she'd been dating had sent gifts to her work before – roses, chocolates… nothing original but nothing that made her feel stupid, either. Because thinking that this had come from Mitch *did* make her feel stupid. Stupid that she'd thought they were so in-tune – that he thought this was the kind of thing that would appeal to her.

She felt a flush of secondhand embarrassment. This is the kind of gift a 15-year old boy gave his girlfriend.

"Am I a total spoiled brat that I don't even care who it's from, I just want it out of my office?" she pulled a face at Becky.

"It's all yours Sar. I don't think you could even palm it off to one of the interns," Becky laughed as she sauntered back to her own desk. "And just so you know, I'm totally Instagraming a photo of you carrying it home."

Two meetings and two cups of coffee later, Sara finally bit the bullet and text Mitch.

Sara: Should I be thanking you for my gift this morning?
Mitch: Which gift is that Princess? The gift of extreme sexual satisfaction?
Sara: I have a large teddy bear sitting on my desk.
Mitch: Did you WANT me to send you a teddy bear?
Sara: No!

Mitch: Good. Because babe, I'm not the teddy bear type.

Sara: Thank god. It's hideous.

Sara: Oh, and PS. You're messaging with the new deputy editor of High Gloss. Squee!

Mitch: Atta girl :)

Sara sat back in her chair, sighing as her chest untightened. She hadn't realized just how worked up this damn bear had made her. Which was ridiculous – who cared if a man she was sleeping with a few times gave her a gift? As tacky and inappropriate as it was, even if it *had* come from Mitch in a week or two it wouldn't matter – their brief fling would be over and she'd be free to get rid of the thing.

Because the only thing she wanted as reminder of her time with Mitch were deliciously toe-curling memories.

Dropping into her desk chair she stared sightlessly at her blank computer screen, struck by the fact that none of her previous encounters with men had given her an indication of just how amazing sex could be. Why was that? She'd done plenty of kissing, hell, even something that resembled second base. And none of that had prepared her for the raw intensity and shivery deliciousness of sex itself.

If she'd known, if she'd even had an inkling, she'd have been on this bandwagon *long* ago. As it was, this afternoon couldn't come quickly enough.

Sara was pissed. She was actually tapping her toe against the floor like a goddamn caricature.

It was late afternoon and the photo shoot at Ink Inc.

had been underway for a good hour. An hour in which the photographer – Kirsty – had been unashamedly throwing herself at Mitch; purring directions and suggestive remarks his way.

If Kirsty hadn't been a long-term freelancer for the magazine who was exceptional at her work, Sara would have been tempted to pull her aside and have a chat about inappropriate behavior.

Instead, she glanced away from the sight of a bare chested Mitch – tattooed skin gleaming under the camera lights set up around him – and took a gulp of water, suppressing the urge to drag Kirsty out by her hair and leap into Mitch's arms herself.

Maybe Kirsty wasn't the only one who needed a lecture on inappropriate behavior.

But oh God, those *arms*. He was curling one arm over his torso, his massive bicep flexing, which sent a corresponding tug of warmth to Sara's core.

She had to remind herself the itching impulse to maim Kirsty wasn't possessiveness over Mitch. It was the fact this story was her baby; *she* was the one pulling this piece together, and she hated handing control of the creative direction to someone else.

It absolutely had nothing to do with re-living how that man's body had felt moving over hers last night. The feel of his clenching buttocks under her fingers as he'd driven deep. Claiming her.

Nope, it was purely professional.

Sitting behind the scenes, she could see each shot as it was taken flashing up on the screen of a laptop and they were good. *Really* good.

Slipping off her heels and tucking her legs beneath her she was attempting to settle – both her body and her emotions – when Kirsty turned her back on Mitch, discreetly flipping open the top button on her blouse, allowing a show of lace-covered cleavage.

Oh hell no you don't, woman.

Before she could think twice, Sara had sprung to her feet and was marching barefoot towards the lit-up area, pushing past the lighting technician and waving away the photography assistant who made to intercept her.

"Okay Kirsty, time for a break!" she chirped with faux brightness, hiding gritted teeth behind a big smile. "I promised Mitch."

"Five more minutes Sara," Kirsty said irritably, not looking away from the lens of her camera. "We're really on a roll here."

As soon as she'd entered their working space Sara had felt the weight of Mitch's gaze, her skin tightening in anticipation.

Straightening up, he rolled his shoulders.

"Actually, I could do with a break," he spoke at Kirsty but had eyes only for Sara, his stare heavy-lidded with barely concealed desire.

"*That* was the shot," muttered Kirsty, continuing to snap photos.

Ignoring her, Mitch stepped out of the lights and stalked towards Sara.

"Fine," sighed Kirsty. "Chelsea, find me a Coke Zero," she directed at her assistant as she headed over to the laptop. Sara knew she'd be dying to go through what she'd taken so far, and it would be at least 20 minutes until shooting resumed.

"Hi," he murmured, coming to a halt mere millimeters

from her. Tipping her head back she just stared, struck anew by the sheer size of him.

"I can't wait to hear what you promised me," he raised an eyebrow and grinned wolfishly at her.

"What?" damn pheromones were clouding her head. And his lips were close, so close. If she just went on tiptoe, and he just leant down a little more…

"You told the photographer you promised me," he reminded her, lowering his head a fraction more.

"Oh, that." She breathed out and the slight exhalation had her chest brushing against his shirtless one. All that smooth skin stretching taut over hard muscle, the swirls of ink, that delectable trail of hair leading beneath his low-slung jeans… without thinking her hands drifted to his denim-covered hips, the tips of her fingers brushing the warm skin of his torso.

"I'll promise whatever you want," she admitted, briefly wondering if this man had somehow drugged her with his nearness. "Just kiss me please."

——

Having Sara ask for his kiss was quite possibly the sweetest thing Mitch had ever heard. She was tiny before him, barefoot and breathy, and he was more than happy to oblige.

She'd obviously forgotten they were surrounded by people she worked with, and he didn't give a damn.

Leaning into him she rose on her tippy toes and he grabbed her waist, lifting her to meet his lips, crushing her to his needy mouth. What was it about her that had him so desperate? It was as though he couldn't ever get close enough. Even last night, when he'd been buried inside her, he wanted more.

The kiss deepened, their breath quickening. She was literally trembling in his arms and he fought to restrain a moan.

Reluctantly pulling his head back he let her slide down his body until her feet touched the floor, even as her kiss-swollen lips silently begged for more.

An image of her on her knees before him, begging with those lips, had his cock pushing painfully against his jeans. Christ, he had to get his head back in the game.

Breathing out he took a step back, running his hand through his hair.

"I'm going to hold you to that promise Princess, but not here."

He could see lust clearing from her eyes and her cheeks heating, as she realised they'd been making out in public. No one appeared to have noticed however, having all crowded around the laptop.

"Come out with me after this," he asked. "We're having staff drinks at a bar downtown."

Blood pumped loudly through his veins as he waited for her response. He was surprised she couldn't hear it.

He was assuming there was an unacknowledged agreement between them that they would continue to see each other, but what if he was wrong? Was chemistry alone enough to convince her to step outside her clearly defined boundaries?

Because it was one thing to give in to their incendiary attraction in private – would she be willing to test-drive their magnetism in his world?

And was he crazy for wanting it so much?

"What if I already have plans?" she asked coyly, and he

knew instantly she didn't.

"It's Monday night Princess, it's a fairly safe bet."

He reached out, wrapping her long ponytail around his fist and gently tugging to tip her face to his. "And I have a promise to collect."

He fixated on the pulse fluttering in her neck, swallowing as he remembered leisurely licking that exact spot last night.

"You two are about to start a fire in here," Jennifer commented dryly, appearing from the kitchenette out the back. "How about we try and keep it professional?" and with a wink she walked past.

The studio had closed for the afternoon to accommodate the shoot, with only Jennifer remaining, and she had taken great pleasure in watching how uncomfortable Mitch was as they prepped him.

He'd been happy to have his hair styled, but firmly drew the line at having a makeup artist rub oil on his chest and arms. When they'd argued it highlighted his ink under the lights he'd relented but insisted on applying it himself, watching Sara the whole time as his hands smoothed it on.

Until she'd bitten her bottom lip and his erection threatened to become obvious. Then he'd focused on getting this over and done with as painlessly as possible.

Which brought him back to now.

"Say yes Princess. And let's get these damn photos finished."

Snapping back to work-mode Sara nodded.

"Okay. I'll go and check where Kirsty is up to."

The shoot went for another hour although Mitch was fairly sure Kirsty had what she needed and was just toying with him. A fact confirmed when she passed him a note with her number on it as they were packing up.

It was inordinately pleasing to see a flash of anger in Sara's eyes as she witnessed the exchange and he smiled to himself as he politely turned the photographer down.

Leaving Sara to supervise the pack up, he wandered over to where Jennifer was shutting down her computer.

"The boys are already at The Surly Wench, asking when we're getting there. You're in for a world of hurt tonight – they're going to milk this modeling thing for all its worth," she teased.

"I'm not modeling, and you know it. And tell them to bring it, I'm a big boy."

"You are such an innate flirt you don't even realize you're doing it," she shook her head. "What's going on with the journalist?"

They both looked over at Sara, who was on the phone with her back to them. *Damn* she had an amazing ass.

Avoiding Jennifer's question, because he genuinely didn't know how to answer, he instead told her that Sara would be joining them at the bar.

She narrowed her eyes speculatively, but didn't say a word.

"What about you?" he asked. "Bringing this new boyfriend I haven't met yet?"

"Actually, he says he has met you. You guys knew each other when you were younger."

"Really? What's his name?"

"Stu. He said you go way back, but didn't really elaborate. I figured he'd go into it when you guys saw each other again," she shrugged.

Mitch couldn't for the life of him remember a Stu. But

his past, especially his early past, was littered with people he wouldn't want Jennifer walking past, let alone having a relationship with. He had a sick feeling in his stomach.

Who the hell is Stu?

"So is he coming out tonight?"

"No, he's working."

"What does he do?"

"What is this – 20 Questions? You're not my big brother Mitch."

Remembering again Simon's unfavourable comments about the guy his jaw clenched. A slither of unease had his spine straightening.

"Well I'd like to meet him. Get him to drop by the studio sometime."

He felt, rather than saw, Sara walk towards them. It was like his body came on high alert whenever she was in the vicinity. The atoms in his body recognized and reacted to the atoms in hers. Or something equally crazy.

All he knew was that his blood pumped harder whenever she was near.

"Hey Jennifer, are you coming out tonight?" Sara stood close enough beside him for their bodies to brush, but otherwise made no move to touch him. Not that it mattered. He could see her nipples tightening into nubs under her silk blouse and knew she was just as affected by his presence.

His throat was suddenly too dry to speak.

"I am pretty lady. I'm going to take a shot in the dark and say you've never been to The Surly Wench before?"

"No, but I think I've heard of it. It's in Surry Hills isn't it?"

Jennifer hummed in agreement, looking Sara over.

"I tell you what Sara. How about you and I do some girly bonding and meet Mitch there?"

"Girly bonding?" Mitch cleared his throat. "Really?"

"We might do an outfit change too. Can you imagine the scene she'd cause walking into the bar dressed like this?" Jennifer grinned in delight at the thought.

"What's wrong with what I'm wearing?" Sara demanded, hands on hips.

Which was when Mitch realized Jennifer had a point. Sara was the epitome of a sexy librarian today, and in that snug pencil skirt and almost-sheer blouse there was a high chance he'd be leaving the Wench with bruised knuckles – he wouldn't be able to help himself if anyone were to be inappropriate.

He sighed.

"You've got an hour Jenn. And then I want my woman at that bar."

"Your woman?" both women asked in unison with matching raised eyebrows.

He smacked a kiss on Jennifer's cheek and then another – lingering one – on Sara's lips.

"One hour ladies."

Because he was heading to the bar by himself he took his bike instead of an uber, the rush of riding almost enough to make up for the absence of Sara. He knew Jimmy, the bar's manager, would let him park the bike out the back for the night so he could still take Sara home later.

Removing his helmet, he sat on the bike's seat and dragged his fingers through his hair. The question of Jennifer's boyfriend's identity was rubbing him the wrong way. Taking out his phone, he dialed Maggie.

"Hey Mags, how's it going?"

"Good big brother. You?"

"About to go into the Wench for a drink. Listen Mags, do you remember Stu?"

"Shit, I didn't think you'd heard."

"Heard what?" his voice cracked in alarm.

"I was talking with Mary, do you remember her?"

Yeah he remembered her. She was his sister's busty friend back in Year 8 that he'd screwed behind the sports shed.

"Uh, yeah?"

"She said that Stuart got out of jail a couple of months ago."

"Who the *fuck* is Stuart?"

"I forgot you guys just called him Wendel. Stuart Wendel."

The line went quiet between them.

Well fuck.

CHAPTER 14

Sara was surprisingly comfortable in Jennifer's company, the other woman had a low-key way of going with the flow that had them easily chatting.

Jennifer had been enthusiastic when Sara suggested calling Marc to join the so-called bonding time, and when there was a knock at Jennifer's front door Sara opened it with a flourish.

"Baby doll, have you started the party without me?" Marc chided, grinning at the drink Sara held aloft.

"We are drinking *whiskey* tonight Marc!" she announced, leading him to Jennifer's bedroom.

"Well hello gorgeous," Marc drawled at Jennifer. "You're almost scrumptious enough to make me rethink my sexuality."

"Your sexuality is the only reason I'm letting a strange man into my bedroom, buster," she replied, looking up from the dressing table mirror where she was meticulously re-applying her eyeliner. "That, and your girl Sara here has vouched for you. Oh, and the fact she said you're a genius with hair. Want to try an old-school victory roll in my hair?"

As Marc styled Jennifer's hair they kept up a steady commentary through the mirror, watching Sara try and discard several dress options from Jennifer's closet.

As Sara did a twirl in a pink blossom jacquard swing dress Jennifer tutted and stood up.

"Nope, too pretty. I want you to blow Mitch's mind

tonight.”

Sara stopped mid twirl and picked up a bottle of coral red Mexican Salsa nail polish sitting on Jennifer’s bedside table.

“Where did you get this?” she asked curiously. “I didn’t think they’d released this yet?”

“What, the polish? Stu gave it to me. It was a kind of strange, out of the blue gift, but whatever. Isn’t the colour divine?”

“Tell me more about this boss of yours Jennifer,” interrupted Marc, taking her seat at the mirror and fluffing his own hair. “I want to know all about the man who’s got my girl forgetting her husband search.”

“Husband search?” Jennifer raised an eyebrow at Sara. “He’s crushing hard on her, and to be honest it’s out of character for him. But he’s definitely not looking for a wife.”

“I’m not *marrying* him,” stressed Sara, taking another long drink from her whiskey and coke. “I’m just fucking him.”

Marc spun around on the vanity stool, his hand raised in exaggerated shock. “Girl, I have *never* heard you use language like that before.”

“What?” Sara was defensive, emptying her glass and reaching for the bottle of Maker’s Mark to refill. “I say fuck.”

“You absolutely do *not* say fuck. I’ve never heard you say fuck.”

“Okay, so maybe I just think it. But I think it a lot.”

“We are going to have fun tonight,” Jennifer laughed, looking between the two of them. “Your waist would look amazing in this,” she held up a fifties-style black rock ‘n’ roll full circle skirt, “but none of my tops are going to fit you properly. We need to find a dress that’s going to work… what about this?” she asked, holding up a dark rose print pencil dress.

"It's gorgeous, but I thought you were trying to steer me away from looking like a librarian?"

"Pretty girl, there's not a chance in hell you're going to look like a librarian when I've finished with you."

The driver couldn't stop eyeing the three of them in the backseat of the taxi, and it wasn't just their whiskey-fueled high spirits.

"Baby doll he is totally digging you," Marc whisper-squealed, digging his elbow into the cropped and fitted black motorcycle jacket that Sara wore over the rose print dress, which totally roughed up the femininity of the outfit.

"And he hasn't even seen you without the jacket," Jennifer was just as gleeful.

"I'm pretty sure I'd scare the fuck out of him if I took the jacket off," replied Sara drily.

Seated on either side of her, Marc and Jennifer reached in front of her to slap a high five. They were still acting like schoolchildren every time she cursed.

"It takes a *man* to handle tats like that on a woman," agreed Jennifer in satisfaction, settling back into the seat.

Sara was buzzing, and it only had a small amount to do with the alcohol as the anticipation of seeing Mitch fizzed through her. She'd let Jennifer have her way with her, and with loosely curled hair hanging down her back, vamp-red lips and matching red satin mule heels, she was feeling sexy.

But that wasn't even the best part.

Jennifer had meticulously applied tattoo transfers in sleeves down both Sara's arms, with a vixen mermaid curling over the top of her right breast – displayed in all its impish glory by the plunging neckline of the dress.

The confidence that came with having metamorphized into this rockabilly chick dissolved any nerves she may have been harbouring about meeting Mitch's friends and work colleagues. She wasn't Sara Morrison tonight. She was just a woman meeting an insanely sexy guy at a bar, and the thought of his face when she revealed her tattooed body had a secret dancing on her lips.

"Tell us about this man of yours," Marc encouraged Jennifer. "You haven't been together long, have you?"

"Just a couple of weeks. I'm not sure if he's just pretending to be a bad boy, or if he really is one, but either way he's got me hooked," she sighed dreamily.

"How'd you meet?" Sara asked, wondering if maybe he was in sales in the beauty industry, or even marketing or PR. How else could he have got that nail polish? It definitely hadn't been launched yet.

"I met him in a bar. He tried to pick me up and I decided to let him. He's aloof and brooding and the sex is out of this world."

"So basically he's a shithead but you're using him for his body?" surmised Marc. "Because if that's the case you're totally selling yourself short."

"You haven't seen his body," Jennifer sighed.

Which was all it took to have Sara heating up at the thought of Mitch's muscled shoulders and defined abs. God, she'd almost come on the spot this afternoon watching as he'd rubbed oil onto his inked skin. It should be illegal for a man to look the way he did.

"So is there going to be anyone here tonight for me to play

with?" asked Marc.

"No one on the team is openly gay, but I'm pretty sure that Jay might swing both ways," mused Jennifer. "Either way, we're going to have fun watching these two pretend they don't have feelings for each other."

"Lust is a feeling Jennifer," Sara replied primly, shoving the other woman's butt as they slid from the back seat of the taxi onto the pavement. "And that is absolutely all there is between Mitch and I. We couldn't be more different if we tried."

"Doesn't look like it tonight," smirked Jennifer, returning the slap on the ass.

The bar was crowded and the air was heavy with humidity and amplified sound. Despite this, Sara immediately located Mitch and, as if sensing her presence he broke off his conversation, swinging to face them as they approached.

"Fuck me." Low and guttural, he sounded pained. "You are actually going to be the death of me Princess." His big hand landed on her hip tugging her to his side. "You look good enough to eat," he murmured in her ear before introducing her to the five men sitting with him.

Still shivering at the hunger in his words, she focused on the seated men as they greeted her – noting their curiosity and grateful when Jennifer and Marc settled around the table and the lively conversation picked back up.

There was not a chance in hell that Sara could concentrate with Mitch pressed against her, his palm sitting low and possessive on her back.

Sara Morrison had no interest in being possessed. But *this*

Sara? She was about to beg for it.

"Your turn to shout drinks Magic Mike," yelled a bulky blonde guy over the music. Sara thought she'd caught his name as Simon.

"I was getting my photo taken, not dancing," Mitch laughed. "You're just jealous no one wants to take photos of your ugly mug."

"I was referring to you stripping, not dancing. And women want photos of other parts of my anatomy," Simon joked, raising suggestive eyebrows at Sara.

"Get your eyes off my woman," Mitch demanded, rolling his eyes. "What can I get you to drink Princess?"

Struggling to tear her attention from Mitch's *seriously* amazing ass as he went to the bar to order a round of drinks, Sara startled as Jennifer nudged her.

"About time you took that jacket off, don't you think?"

"Let's hope it doesn't completely freak him out," Sara replied, shrugging out of the leather and placing it on the stool behind her.

She didn't realize the table had fallen silent until she swung back around.

"Uh, wow," muttered Simon. "That was unexpected. And hot. Very hot."

Suddenly self-conscious, Sara wrapped her arms over her front, her fingertips running over the ink transfer.

"And I'm taking all the credit," Jennifer asserted, throwing an arm over Sara's shoulders. At the quizzical looks, she explained. "It's not real ink. I did some transfers. Look realistic though, don't they?"

"Holy shit, they totally look real," agreed Simon. "Has Mitch seen this?"

"Seen what?" asked the man in question, setting the drinks tray on the table. The seconds stretched with each heavy beat of Sara's heart as his eyes connected with hers, widening in shock as they slid down her body.

It was only the blistering heat in his eyes that saved the sight of his jaw dropping from being comical. As it was, the heat from his stare was enough to ignite a burning ache between her legs, his blatant hunger sweeping away her earlier nerves.

This version of Sara was ready for whatever he had to bring.

———

Mitch had been waiting for an opening to have a private chat with Jennifer. The news that Wendel was out of jail and *dating her* had his gut churning. Yes, the man may have served his sentence and repaid his debt to society, but no amount of time behind bars was going to get that particular tiger to change his stripes.

He needed Jennifer to know Wendel's true nature.

Returning from the bar he was preoccupied, and hence grateful he'd placed the drinks tray on the table before he looked over at Sara. Because his world tilted off its axis.

He was used to thinking with his dick. And while it didn't always have great sense, it always guaranteed a good time. The problem was, around Sara it wasn't just his dick that responded and demanded. It was his whole damn body.

While he could be counted on to have a hard on the majority of the time he spent in her company, his skin was hyper-sensitive to her nearness, his heart rate kicked into overdrive when he caught her scent and, worst of all, she was in his head.

All the fucking time.

Which all of a sudden didn't matter, not one little fucking bit, because coherent thought ceased to exist the moment she shed that sexy-as-fuck leather jacket and revealed those ink covered arms. And her divinely sculpted shoulders. And a *mermaid* on her *tit*.

He hadn't realized his shock had created an absence of sound until it rushed back at him, the boys pissing themselves laughing at his slack jaw.

Shaking himself, he stalked around the table and wedged himself between her barstool and the high-top table, his broad back effectively blocking most of the ribbing that was coming his way.

The smack talk didn't register. They didn't register.

"Are you going caveman in public?" He was so close that Sara's head was tilted back in order to speak to him, her chest rising and falling rapidly and those red lips of hers softly parted.

He would sell his motorcycle right now if he could have those lips wrapped around his cock.

"Do you *want* me to go caveman in public?"

Reaching out, his finger grazed the mermaid that accentuated the swell of her breast, thrilling at the goosebumps that broke out along her arms.

Turning his attention to them, his palms smoothed up each arm, appreciating the delicately applied transfers and the way they turned his princess into a god damn warrior queen.

"Jennifer did this?"

"Uh huh. You like?"

"I like." There was a rough quality to his voice that didn't dissipate even when he cleared his throat. He could feel his throbbing heart in every pulsing inch of his body and if he didn't get his mouth on hers *right now* he was liable to burst a vein.

"Take a seat boss, and admire my handiwork," interrupted Jennifer. "Because I just made this beautiful woman smoking hot."

"She was already smoking hot," but that was low and intimate, meant for Sara's ears only as he took the stool beside her, lodging his thigh against hers beneath the table.

Curbing the desire to devour her was a sharply sweet torture, and for the next hour he managed to converse and laugh with his friends, all the while drinking beer with his left hand because his right was securely between her legs.

Her lace top thigh-high stockings were driving him wild, as minute by minute her clamped thighs slowly relaxed to allow higher exploration.

Drifting out of the conversation, he concentrated on reaching his fingers higher, intent on reaching the warmth of her panties. Releasing a breathy sigh, she finally allowed her legs to slacken completely and he couldn't help a grin of triumph from flashing across his face.

Catching it, her own face reddened and she ducked her head, that glossy hair of hers providing a measure of privacy to her mounting arousal.

Absently, he wondered how long they could continue this charade of social propriety as his finger breached the lace of her panties and found the delicious heat of her pussy.

Her friend Marc was hilarious and had quickly become the

life of the party, but he was also observant as fuck, watching Mitch with knowing eyes.

Not even knowing eyes could stop this.

Sara squirmed and her sleekly muscled thighs contracted as his finger slid along her folds, reveling in her slick wetness. Finding the nub of her clit he circled it, lost wholly in the sight of her hiding a moan behind her hand.

But when she bit the pad of her own thumb in a bid to restrain herself, he lost it. Withdrawing from the sanctity of her body he stood up so fast that the stool almost toppled.

"Time to go Princess," he growled, tugging her off her own stool. Throwing a "see you tomorrow" over his shoulder he turned to leave, impatient for privacy.

"Wait!" she protested, tugging ineffectually on his hand. "Jennifer, thank you so much. And Marc, I'll call you tomorrow."

"Do you want me to throw you over my shoulder?" he threatened her.

She was flushed and flustered and altogether delicious.

Willing and wordless, she allowed him to usher her in front of his body and out the back door. He'd had too much to drink to ride his motorcycle, but there wasn't a chance in hell he was going to wait out the front for an uber, and then the trip home, without slaking his hunger for her first.

The thump of base from inside was still audible, and streetlights from the road behind cast a low glow over the staff parking lot that was empty of everything save his motorcycle and several vehicles. Backing her into a darkened corner beside stacked and empty cardboard boxes he couldn't help the primitive noise that rumbled from his chest.

"Did you just growl at me?" she breathed, pressing her

body against his and reaching up to clasp her hands behind his neck.

He didn't bother to respond. There was no time for words. As need hammered through him he slid hands beneath her dress, raising the hem as he reached her luscious ass and lifted her, forcing her thighs to spread and lock around his waist.

A needy mewl left her lips as she instinctively ground herself against him, and he knew her ache was as great as his.

His hands spanning and kneading her ass, he finally, *finally* dropped his mouth to hers, sucking on her bottom lip until she opened to him on a sigh. The softness of her lips, the distinct taste of whiskey, the *rightness* of her tongue rubbing his left him short of breath.

It was a shamelessly desperate kiss; Mitch was drowning as his mouth ravaged hers.

"I'm going to fuck you against this wall Princess. Right here, in public. I'm going to hitch this dress up and pull your panties aside and push into your pussy. I'm going to fuck you hard and you're going to love it. You're going to scream my name as I make you come. Because you're in my world, and you don't look like a princess tonight. Tonight you're my woman and I'll take you however I want."

She stilled, eyes wide on his.

Was it too much, too strong? He wouldn't take it back even if he could. She joked about his being a caveman but the truth was, she *made* him this way.

He reveled in the weight of her in his arms, in the sting of his scalp as she twined her fingers into his hair. And he didn't give a damn if someone ventured out here and saw him claiming his woman.

"I can't fuck you, out here," she stammered, catching her bottom lip between her teeth.

"Why not?"

He pushed her ass tighter against him, forcing her core to fit more snuggly against him. In reaction, her head dropped back against the wall, baring her throat to his rapacious lips.

He licked and sucked down the milky skin of her neck, breathing deep her drugging vanilla scent. Jesus he needed to be inside her.

"Wait. Mitch, we need to slow down," she brought her head off the wall grabbed his face in her hands, forcing his eyes to meet hers.

"I look like someone else tonight, but I'm still me. A new outfit and transfer tattoos don't change who I am on the inside. And I don't fuck against walls in public."

He rocked his pelvis against her and she groaned.

"No matter how much I want it."

"Don't you want me as much as I want you?" he ground out.

"More. But I'm not doing this here." Her palms cradled his face, softening her words. "Women might do this kind of thing in your world, but not in mine."

He buried his face in her neck in defeat. He actually didn't think he could walk with his cock as hard as it currently was. He was wound so tight it was hard to breathe.

"Okay Princess. Okay."

Releasing her ass, she unwound her legs and slid down his body.

He couldn't step back. Couldn't put distance between their pressed bodies.

"Show me your world then Princess. Show me how we

can be together in your world."

"What?" She was confused.

A chill skated over him that had nothing to do with the temperature. What had he just said? And did he care that he was putting himself on the line?

"My people have seen me with you. Are you afraid to let your people see you with me?"

CHAPTER 15

"Are you afraid to let your people see you with me?"

Sara tossed in her bed, alone, Mitch's words chasing themselves on an endless loop through her head. Groaning she sat up, clutching a pillow to her chest.

She'd been on a high fueled by lust and whiskey and when Mitch had challenged her she'd freaked the hell out. Like, proper freaked. She'd turned tail and fled around the side of the bar to the front, where she'd hailed a conveniently passing taxi.

Looking back out the window, she'd seen Mitch standing helplessly on the sidewalk, hands running through his hair in what looked like frustration.

Regret was a solid, heavy presence in her stomach, with anxiety fluttering madly around it. Struggling to make sense of her tangled emotions she slipped on her glasses and padded to the kitchen, flicking on the kettle.

Not that a cup of tea was likely to solve this. How late was too late to call Sophie?

Screw it, best friends are available 24/7.

Settling into the sofa with a mug of chamomile tea, Sara dialed Sophie and hoped like hell she'd answer, even thought it was almost midnight.

"Are you okay?" Sophie's concern was evident even through her sleepy voice.

"I'm fine. It's an emotional emergency."

"So you're at home, and safe?" Sophie clarified.

"Well, there isn't an axe murderer beneath my bed, but I'm not safe from my thoughts. I'm on some kind of emotional roller coaster and I feel like my head is going to explode."

Which wasn't far from the truth. Her whole world had sped up since she'd met Mitch, and the heightened emotions he brought out in her made the crazy whirl that much crazier.

"Is this about having sex with Mitch?" asked Sophie gently.

"No. Yes. It's everything Soph. I feel like I'm out of control," she admitted. "It's all so confusing. I've literally known Mitch for two seconds, but I have these insanely intense feelings for him and I don't know if they're really for him, or just because I've discovered how awesome sex is and I'm in love with lust, you know?"

"You're in love?"

"No! No, I'm definitely not in love. Definitely. God Soph, he is *not* the type of guy I'm going to fall in love with."

"How sure are you about that Sar? Because I've never known you to get so worked up. Maybe he's pushing you outside your comfort zone, and that's a good thing. Because I've got to be honest, I was getting kind of worried about how set you were on your Husband Hunt, I feel like maybe you're just trying to please your parents?"

A flash of denial had Sara tightening her fingers around the mug of tea, before she silently acknowledged the truth of the matter and relaxed.

"Were you judging me for trying to find a husband?" she asked quietly.

"No! Absolutely not! I want you to be happy Sar, however that happens. I'm just worried you're placing too much pressure on yourself," Sophie quickly assured her. "God I wish I was there now to give you a hug and open a bottle of vodka."

"I'm pretty sure eight-month pregnant women should not drink vodka Soph."

"Who said I was drinking? I was going to get you drunk and when you passed out draw a moustache on you."

They both laughed, and Sara closed her eyes. *God* she missed her best friend.

"When do I get to see you again?" she asked.

"Well considering you're going to be this baby's godmother, I'm hoping it'll be as soon as its born," replied Sophie.

Tears pricking her eyes, Sara covered her mouth and squealed.

"Really? You really want to entrust the spiritual guidance of your child to me?"

"Yes Sara, I do," Sophie said seriously.

Sobering, Sara took a deep breath. Seeing as they were going deep and meaningful, maybe she could ask, and be brave enough to hear Sophie's answer.

"Soph, do you think I'm a horrible, shallow person for not even considering that Mitch could be potential husband material? I mean, I barely know him, so obviously I'm not ready to marry the guy, but I haven't even been open to the possibility of the potential."

"You're not a horrible person honey, forget that right now. I think you've allowed yourself to narrow your vision – thinking that happy only comes in a certain kind of package. I've got nothing against your parents, but I kind of feel that they've pushed you in this direction and, at the end of the day, you need to really think about what makes *you* happy."

They sat quietly for a while, until Sara head the rustle of bedlinen and a soft mumble from Robert. A sharp jolt of sadness lodged in her chest at the thought of Sophie lying warm and content beside the love of her life. In comparison, her empty apartment and cold bed became unbearably lonely.

"Go back to sleep Soph, sorry for waking you."

"Anytime honey, you know that."

"I know, thank you. Good night."

Not wanting to face her bed and concede the loneliness, Sara instead put down her phone and curled into the sofa, pulling a throw blanket over herself. If she didn't move, maybe she could ignore the ache that was seeping through her body.

But in the quiet of the night, she couldn't deny she missed Mitch. And it wasn't just that she wanted his hot kisses and warm body pressed against her. She missed *him*. His vitality and masculinity, his wit and the way he looked at her like she was the most delicious item on a dessert menu. The way he listened to her, *really* listened to her, and saw not just the well-connected Easter Suburbs blonde that so many previous men had been attracted to.

She could almost taste the regret of walking away from him tonight, it was so visceral. Was she so anxious about how others perceived her that she wouldn't even give herself a chance at finding happiness?

Did it even matter what anyone else thought? Hell, before meeting Robert, Sophie had been feted by the social pages as one half of Sydney's most coveted It Couple – engaged to a charismatic business mogul who was now languishing in jail. At the end of the day, appearances didn't matter.

And, as much as her stomach flipped to think of her parents coming face to face with Mitch, was that worth risking the chance at happiness that he could represent? As she finally fell asleep, Sara knew she should at least give him the opportunity to try fitting into her world before deciding it wasn't going to work. Because honestly, it wasn't like he was a monster.

———

"Are you fucking kidding me?" Spitting out the takeaway coffee, Mitch all but threw the cup back onto the front counter of Ink Inc. "This has enough sugar in it to put a diabetic into a coma," he snapped at Jennifer.

"Don't lose your shit at me, I just collected the order – I didn't place it or make it," she shot back at him. "And I know tattoo artists have a reputation for being bad ass, but you need to pull yourself together before you start scaring clients away." Giving him a pointed look, she turned to answer the phone.

It didn't matter that he knew she was right, his black mood was bleeding all over. Ever since he'd monumentally fucked up with Sara last night, his life had been falling apart. From having a fight with Maggie and then "accidentally" breaking his laptop, to having a client he'd blocked out three hours to work on cancel, nothing was going his way. Not to mention he was still processing that Wendel was out of jail and what the possible ramifications of that could be… and now to top it all off, his caffeine hit had been ruined with sugar.

Abandoning the offending beverage he stalked back to

his tattoo room, closing the door forcefully behind him. Dropping onto the stool he lowered his head into his hands, holding back a groan.

He'd come on too strong with Sara last night, and she'd walked out on him. Just left. And hell, could he even blame her? She joked about him being a Viking, but the reality of his uncensored needs had sent her running. Literally.

For fuck's sake, she was a virgin less than 24 hours earlier, and he'd been ready to ravage her against the back wall of a pub, modesty be damned. He'd been so *stupid*.

Talk about thinking with your dick.

Compounding his self-flagellation was a hard ball of hurt that seemed stuck at the back of his throat. He'd never been self-conscious of who he was – as a teenager he didn't have the self-awareness, and ever since he'd known there was more to life than street gangs he'd been determined to better his situation. If he ever thought about it, which was rare, he was proud of what he'd achieved.

He'd come from nothing, his mother had over-dosed when he was 17 and he'd never known his father. Yet here he was, living his dream and running a successful business. The fact that Sara knew he wasn't good enough for her cut deep. Not that he hadn't already known, but her thinking it hurt a lot worse than he'd imagined it would.

He'd been fooling himself. Because the thought of introducing him into her world was obviously so repugnant that it wasn't even worth discussing. And considering she didn't even know the worst of it, maybe that was for the best.

A tentative knock on the door caused him to start. Pulling his mind from that long-ago night he raised his head, watching as Jennifer entered the room.

"I know this is probably not great timing, but Stu is here and you said you wanted to meet him…" she trailed off, her brow lowering with concern as she noticed the defeated slump of Mitch's shoulders. "Actually, don't worry – "

Mitch cut her off. "Stu?"

"My new boyfriend."

"Yeah, I knew who you meant."

Mitch cursed inwardly. He hadn't yet spoken to Jennifer about Wendel and now his hand was being forced without him having the time to decide how he was going to approach this. He didn't want Jennifer to shoot the messenger, but she had to be told.

"Cool, he's in the kitchenette." Jennifer was already backing through the doorway.

Anxiety and adrenaline had Mitch pushing to his feet. He'd known the day would come when his past would re-surface, and it looked like today was the day.

"Wait, Jenn!" But she'd already left.

Following her to the kitchenette at the back of the studio, Mitch kept his steps even and a purposefully blank look on his face. Maybe this was nothing more than an old friend trying to re-connect.

And maybe the earth was fucking flat.

Slowing as he entered the room he fought to control the frown threatening to reveal his feelings. Jennifer sashayed into the waiting arms of a man who'd spent the last decade in jail for violently beating a kid to death.

Not this his fists had been the only ones causing damage.

"Long time no see Mitch," said Stu Wendel, wrapping his arms possessively around Jennifer and tugging her close. Looking over Jennifer's head he locked eyes with Mitch, smirking. "Bet you couldn't wait to catch up with me."

Feigning nonchalance, Mitch leaned back against the door and hoped like hell his clenched jaw wasn't noticeable. The idea of Wendel having his hands anywhere near Jennifer made his stomach roll.

The man was dangerous, a manipulating and reckless sociopath. As kids Mitch had found Wendel with a stray cat bailed up in an alley. He'd confronted him about the mutilated small animals that were sporadically found stuffed into neighbourhood mailboxes but Wendel had denied it. He always had a story. But even when his stories were plausible, they couldn't ever dispel Mitch's gut feeling that a rotting badness pervaded Wendel's core.

"Wendel." He dipped his chin in acknowledgment.

"What? Not even a handshake for an old friend?" Wendel's grin was predatorily lazy. "Ah, don't worry brother. I've got my hands full with this one anyway."

Jennifer turned in the embrace to face Mitch, her sharp eyes curious.

"What is up with you today Mitch?" she demanded.

"Didn't you hear he had a fight with his little lady last night?" Wendel asked with a knowing chuckle.

"What happened with Sara?" Jennifer pulled herself from Wendel's arms and took a step towards Mitch, before spinning back to Wendel. "Wait, how did *you* know about it? I am so freakin' confused right now." She looked between the two men, sensing the tension. "Is that Simon hollering my name? Give me a second, I need to see what's going on out the front."

With Jennifer gone, Mitch clenched and unclenched his fists, advancing on Wendel until only a few feet separated them.

"You got some muscle on you, brother. I'm impressed," drawled Wendel, eyeing Mitch up and down but not backing away. "But while I was inside, I did a few weights myself."

"What do you know about last night?" Mitch growled. The thought of Wendel's eyes on Sara had his skin crawling.

"Just checking the lay of the land, brother. I've got a business proposition to discuss with you."

"I'm not your brother."

"Oh come on Mitch. I went to jail for you. If that doesn't make us brothers, I don't know what does." Wendel's voice was low and sly.

"I *told* you to back off. I told you it was enough. But you wouldn't stop." Mitch ground out, his memory pinging with the metallic scent of blood.

"The fucker tried to rape your *sister* Mitch. He deserved everything he got."

"He didn't deserve to die. I *told* you to stop."

The weight of that night hung heavy in the air. Mitch had been the one to lead the attack, he'd laid the first blow. And, knowing they'd gone too far, he'd fled with Simon as Wendel had continued to kick and punch. It hadn't been about exacting justice for Wendel. He hadn't even really known Maggie. No, for him it was just an opportunity to revel in blood lust.

He could have tried harder to stop Wendel. He could have called for help, and maybe that kid would have survived. But he hadn't, and he had to live with that decision.

When Wendel was arrested for the murder, neither he nor Simon stepped forward. And Wendel didn't utter a word against them.

"You owe me Mitch. And you know it."

"What do you want?" he asked heavily.

"Just a little help in moving some product, that's all."

Oh man, he was so smooth. And it was so not fucking happening.

"No." Mitch was firm. "Not happening."

"I think you should reconsider. You've got the perfect set-up here, and it's good quality gear. We could both make a lot of money."

Stepping closer to Wendel, Mitch looked down at the other man, their chests almost touching. "I said no."

He didn't move an inch, even when Jennifer breezed back into the room, coming to an abrupt stop.

"*What* is going on here?" Her hands hitched on her hips in exasperation. "Mitch, back the fuck away from my boyfriend. I don't care what kind of history you two have, you have no right to behave like this. Seriously!"

"I don't want you seeing him anymore," Mitch rumbled, turning slowly and blocking Jennifer's view of Wendel.

"Well it's too bad you don't get a say in the matter," Jennifer retorted. "Come on Stu, it's my lunch break and we're out of here."

"Wait, we need to talk Jenn," Mitch stepped forward towards her, his hands raised imploringly. "That came out wrong, I'm not trying to tell you what to do."

"Really? Because that's sure what it sounded like," she retorted tartly.

Stu moved from behind Mitch and strolled to Jennifer, his arm snaking around her waist. "It's all good baby girl. No issue here. Mitch and I were just catching up on old times, weren't we brother?"

"I'm not your brother."

"You're being an asshole Mitch, and I'm out of here,"

snapped Jennifer, spinning and walking away.

"Don't come back here," Mitch warned to Wendel's back as he followed.

"Later man." Wendel threw a careless wave in the air without turning around, his hand holding a phone that chirped a message had been sent.

Mitch's phone alerted him to an incoming message and he pulled it from his pocket distractedly before flinching, the air leaving his lungs in a rush. It was a text from an unknown number with no message save for a grainy photo taken in low lighting. A grainy photo taken behind The Surly Wench of Sara's bare legs wrapped around his waist, her head flung back and his head buried in her neck.

Fuck. Fuck fuck fuck.

CHAPTER 16

Sara perched on a stool in her childhood kitchen, sipping a cup of tea and watching the finishing touches for the charity dinner come together. Her mother's efficiency was seriously impressive.

"Right. I just need to finalize the seating arrangements and confirm with the florist when they'll be setting up the displays," she said with satisfaction. "Sara you've been an amazing help on the committee – we all really appreciate your contribution."

"It's been fun to watch you in your element," she teased, internally admitting that it had also been a great distraction from obsessing over Mitch.

They hadn't seen or spoken to each other in almost a week.

Outwardly, Sara was keeping it together. Inside? Not so much. At least a hundred times a day she debated calling him. It was insane how much she missed him. But he hadn't been in touch with her either, and that stung.

"Now, I've kept a plus one ticket for you, are you planning on bringing anyone?" her mother's question interrupted her brooding.

Taking a sip of tea to give herself some time, Sara slowly set the mug back onto the stone countertop. Without looking at her mother, she nodded.

"There is someone I was thinking of inviting." Finally she made eye contact. "But he's not my usual type of date, and I don't want you to freak out."

"Honey, why on earth would I "freak out", as you so eloquently put it?"

Sara couldn't help a grin as her mother held up her fingers in quotation marks when she repeated "freak out".

"He's just different, that's all."

"What? Does he have a membership to the Rosebay Yacht Club instead of the Royal Sydney?"

"He doesn't come from money, he's, he's a self-made businessman."

"Self-made?" her mother sniffed, as though it were a dirty word. "What on earth does he do Sara?"

"He's an artist," Sara replied, proud of herself that it wasn't really a lie. "And very successful."

"But I haven't heard of him? Doubtful he could be as successful as you think darling. Nevertheless, I look forward to meeting this young man."

Now I just have to get him to agree to come.

Clutching the magazine page proofs to her chest, Sara was somewhat reassured she had a legitimate reason to be calling into Ink Inc.

Oh who was she kidding? She was pretty sure Mitch wouldn't give a damn what his feature in the magazine looked like. It was more a matter of how he'd react when she showed up after almost a week of silence.

It was ridiculous how often she found herself loitering out the front of his business. Shaking back her loose hair she mentally pulled her big girl panties up and walked through the front door.

"I was wondering when we'd see your pretty face again," drawled Jennifer in greeting. "I do some of the best makeover work of my life, and then nothing. Nada." In a signature move she raised her eyebrow, elbows on the counter and chin in hands. "Seriously girl, where have you been? Mitch has been a bear with a sore head all week."

At a loss to explain the situation, Sara just smiled. "You wouldn't believe how long the transfers lasted, they were seriously ah-may-zing. One of my friends at work is pregnant and she actually peed in her pants a little when she saw them, thinking it was real."

"Well I do need to book you in with Mitch to get a tattoo, maybe you need to reconsider the size you want," Jennifer grinned.

Sara laughed. "Not a chance!"

Sobering, Jennifer inclined her head towards the closed door to Mitch's tattoo room. "I'm not kidding about the bear with a sore head part. He's been impossible all week. I've quit twice already."

"It can't be too bad, you're still here."

"Only just. Go and see for yourself," Jennifer dared.

"I'm going to cough really loudly if I need you to rescue me," she said, squaring her shoulders and heading towards the room.

"Not a chance girlfriend. You're on your own with this one."

Knocking gently on the door, Sara waited for the gruff "come in" before she cracked the door open. Swallowing, she opened it all the way and stepped inside, closing it gently behind her.

Mitch's broad back was to her and she drank in the sight

of his thick neck and muscled shoulders, the sheer damn *size* of him. He was working at a table, a large sketch pad spread in front of him as his hand moved swiftly across it.

"This better be good Jenn – I told you I didn't want to be disturbed," he growled.

Sara winced, wishing she'd taken the time to come up with some opening words. With the silence about to get uncomfortable, she realized she should just go with the truth.

"I've missed you," she said quietly.

Mitch's hand stilled, his back tensed. And then before she could take another breath he was standing before her, tugging her against his chest.

And *oh man* it felt good to be in his arms.

Holding her so tightly she could feel the steady thump of his heart, his hands stroking firmly up and down her back, he dropped his head to nuzzle in her hair.

"Fuck, Sara. *Sara*." He all but groaned, and she felt it all the way to her core. Yep, her lady parts had missed the shit out of him too.

"I'm sorry I ran out on you without talking," she mumbled into his shirt. "That wasn't fair on you. It all just got a bit overwhelming and –."

"It was my fault, I came on too strong," he cut her off. "*Fuck*. I'm just so glad you're here," he breathed, pulling back to look down at her as one big hand rose, pushing strands of her hair behind her ear. "Thank you for coming to me Princess."

"If I hadn't, would you have come to me?" she asked, surprised by how much she needed to know the answer. If she was going to go all in with this relationship, she wanted to know where he stood.

"I don't know," he admitted, a pained expression on his face. "You were probably right to leave me. I understand why you wouldn't want to introduce me to your world. I know I'm not good enough for you." He didn't meet her eyes.

'What? No! I've never thought you weren't good enough for me!" she exclaimed, standing on tip toes so she could reach for his face, tugging to tilt his chin down so he was forced to look at her. "It's not that you're not good enough, it's just that we're so *different*. And I've been stupidly caught up in what I think I *should* be doing that I didn't see what was right in front of me. We're different, but we fit together. We're right together. You feel it too, I *know* you do. Mad chemistry, right?"

"Yeah, mad chemistry," he conceded. "But that doesn't change the fact that I won't fit into your world, Princess." His eyes were sad and her heart clenched.

"How many men in your social circle have tats like this? How many of them grew up practically on the street? How many didn't go to college? Because that's me, babe. That's who I am and while I'd do *anything* for you, I can't change that."

"I don't want you to change," she said adamantly. "We can make this work. Don't you at least want to try?"

She could see the conflict he was struggling with, and the hopeful butterflies in her stomach sank with dread.

But damnit, he said he'd do anything.

"Is it not worth at least *trying* to make it work?" She couldn't keep the hurt from her voice. "Because if you feel even half of what I feel for you, then you can't walk away from this Mitch. You can't walk away from us."

His chest brushed against hers as he took a deep breath,

his eyes fierce. "If we do this Princess, you need to be sure. Because once we're together, I won't ever be able to walk away. Do you get that? I am in love with you. I am damn *obsessed* with you."

And just like that, Sara understood how heroines in romance novels swooned. How could she not swoon with this Viking warrior of a man professing he *loved* her. He. Loved. Her. Holy crap. He loved her.

"You love me?" She was breathy and feverish and those butterflies in her stomach had got themselves some Redbull.

"Yes Sara, I love you."

And he kissed her. Dear god could the man kiss. She was senseless, clinging to him as his mouth claimed hers with passion and possession and longing. It was everything.

How had she ever walked away from this?

Breathing heavily they broke apart, grinning at each other.

"So if you love me, you couldn't possibly refuse to come to a black tie charity dinner with me, right?"

His grin turned wry. "And miss the opportunity to hang out with the clean skin, educated social elite? Of course not."

——

Mitch wasn't feeling quite so confident as he exited the taxi on Saturday evening. The venue for the dinner was an impressive structure with marble columns and hundreds of fairy lights twinkling from enormous Plane trees standing guard at the entrance. A steady stream of well-heeled guests were walking up the front steps, greeting each other with easy familiarity.

The fact that Sara had invited him into her world made him feel indomitable. Nevertheless, he wished Sara was on his arm. She'd asked him to meet her there as she had needed to arrive early to fulfill her committee obligations and while he understood, he also knew the stakes were high.

As much as Sara insisted it was ridiculous to think he wasn't good enough for her, he needed to navigate tonight successfully – he had no intention of giving her any reason to change that opinion.

And hell, he knew he looked the part. His bespoke tux was handmade by the same tailor that George Clooney frequented, and it covered all his inked skin. And even though Sara had mentioned it was a stand-up cocktail event, he'd had Maggie search YouTube for cutlery etiquette, just in case. So long as no one wanted to discuss trust funds or economic trends, he would be fine.

No, his real concern was Wendel, who was a constant itch at the back of his neck. Jennifer was still dirty with him because of his insistence she break things off with Stu and she refused point blank to talk about the situation. However, it was the photo that Wendel had taken of him with Sara that was viciously eating away at him.

With Sara's experience of compromising photographs he knew she would be upset, and rightly so. He hated that his past could taint her in any way. But more than that, the photo came with an implied theat. Mitch was terrified Wendel would use Sara's safety as leverage, in order to get him to agree to sell the drugs.

He needed to come clean to Sara, and soon. She needed to know the truth.

But tonight wasn't the night for confessions. Tonight was

for showing Sara he could be worthy of her. Shaking off the past, he strode forward.

An elegantly dressed woman of indeterminate age stood as hostess, checking the gold embossed tickets as guests entered. She turned to Mitch expectantly, her lips curved up in greeting.

"Ticket?" she enquired.

"I'm a guest of Sara Morrison, she said she'd leave my ticket at the front," he answered easily.

She perked with renewed interest, inquisitive eyes blatantly taking him in from polished shoes to carefully styled hair.

"Ah, I'd heard our Sara was bringing a date tonight," she murmured. "What did you say your name was?"

"I didn't. It's Mitch, Mitch Smith. And it's a pleasure to meet you." He dipped his head in a charming manner.

Taking his leave he grabbed a flute of champagne from the tray of a passing waiter and looked around the ballroom, his eyes bypassing the crowd to zero in on the vision of perfection that was Sara.

Her delicate collarbones were emphasized by a dusky pink strapless gown that hugged her torso before flowing into a frothy mass of skirt that swept the floor. The colour of the gown was the exact shade of her nipples, and Mitch's throat went dry.

As if sensing his approach she looked up, her face lighting as she moved into his embrace.

"Wow, you look *really* good in a tux." Stepping back she looked him and down, turning his blood hot and his cock hard. "We are definitely attending more functions where you have to get dressed up. I want to eat you."

"That can be arranged."

"Well?" she raised an eyebrow and pouted playfully at him. "Aren't you going to tell me I look nice?"

"You don't look nice, Sara. You look incredible." Ducking his head he whispered huskily at her ear. "You look like a princess and I want to fuck you in the worst way."

"That can be arranged," she repeated his words back at him. "It just so happens that as a committee member, I have all sorts of access and there's a certain room that I think you might really like."

The sassy glint in her eye had him grinning.

"That doesn't sound very responsible Ms Committee Member. Don't you have official duties?"

"Nope, I'm all finished for the night. Come on Mr Smith, follow me," she cajoled, taking his hand in her small one and tugging him behind her.

Stopping briefly to swap his empty champagne flute for two full ones, they were soon slipping through back hallways, past a bustling and brightly lit kitchen and then countless closed doors.

"You do know where you're going, right?" he questioned her, arms snaking out to clasp around her waist, drawing her delicious ass tight against his aching cock. "Because I don't know how much further I can go before I ravish you."

Wordlessly she reached to her left and twisted a door handle, opening it to reveal a small, dim room furnished only with heavy velvet drapes and an empty desk.

"Ravish away, Mr Smith," she breathed, turning in his embrace and linking her hands behind his neck. Obligingly, he lowered his head so she could reach his lips, kissing her hungrily as she walked backwards into the room. She was soft and luscious, the scent of roses and the sweet taste of champagne clouding his head.

Breaking the kiss he closed and locked the door, removing his tux jacket.

"No one's going to find us, don't worry," she promised, urging him to turn once more to face her. "God Mitch, I want you so much. I *need* you."

His chest swelled, his heart throbbing. He loved this woman beyond reason. Guiding her towards the desk he sat on the edge, his long legs bracketing her as she stood between his thighs. Like this, their height difference was negligible. Cupping her face with his large hands he sank into her mouth, licking and nipping and *owning* her. She gave a soft moan of loss when he released her lips, licking down to the pulse fluttering at her throat and sinking his teeth into a gentle bite. Her hands were restless in his hair, urging him on. Finding the zipper at the back of her dress he lowered it enough to allow the strapless bodice to fall around her waist, revealing her perfect tits in all their glory.

"Your body is goddamn holy," he muttered roughly, hands palming her breasts before sucking a pebbled nipple into his starving mouth. Tonguing her taut peak, he used his hands to plump and squeeze, sucking her further in and then biting down to the point of almost-pain.

"Fuck! Mitch!" She arched her back to thrust her tit further into his mouth. "More, please," she begged.

Replacing his mouth with seeking, softly pinching fingers, he moved to her other breast and sucked that nipple deep, feeling her responding moan deep in his balls. Fumbling, he adjusted his straining cock into a more comfortable position, Sara's lust-drugged eyes tracking the movement.

"Remember I said you looked good enough to eat?" she

whispered, sinking to her knees before him.

Mitch stopped breathing, his lungs seizing. The sight of Sara, bare breasted with her voluminous skirt spread on the floor around her, on her knees with her soft lips parted, was the most beautiful thing he'd ever seen. The power she held over him in this moment was breathtaking.

"Princess, are you sure?"

In answer, she unbuckled his belt and sucked on her bottom lip, lowering the zipper of his suit pants. Tugging his cock free she gazed up at him from beneath lowered eyelashes. "I've been wanting to do this for so long," she admitted. "Ever since we first had sex, and I tasted you after you masturbated on me. That was so fucking hot. I dream about that, you know."

He groaned low and long, sucking in a sharp breath as she closed around his cock, gently sucking the crown deep into the warmth of her mouth. Bracing her hands on his thighs she bobbed her head, forcing his cock to touch the back of her throat. Gagging, she pulled back, a string of saliva and pre-cum on her lips. Expecting her to stop, he choked on a shout as she sucked back down his shaft, the warm suction of her mouth an exquisite torture. Using her small hand to fist the base of his cock, she lavished attention on the end, sucking it like a damn lollipop before flattening her tongue and licking him from root to tip, gazing at him with hot eyes.

His knuckles whitened as he gripped the edge of the desk, fighting the primitive urge to rock his hips and push into her. To fuck her mouth. Because she was the one in charge here, and he was damn well going to enjoy going along for the ride.

Humming, she swirled her tongue on the sensitive spot

beneath his dick where the head met the shaft, and he gasped.

"Yeah Princess, like that." He couldn't resist threading his fingers through her silky hair. "So good baby."

Working her mouth in conjunction with her hand she built a rhythm that had his whole body shuddering towards climax. He could feel the pressure building at the base of his spine, his balls heavy with need and his vision blackening.

Her hands grasped the back of his thighs, pushing him firmly into her as she eagerly took his release, swallowing and sucking and swallowing some more.

His harsh breathing finally slowed, and she released his cock with a soft pop, sitting back on her heels and smiling shyly up at him.

"Good?" She asked quietly.

"Earthshattering," he replied.

CHAPTER 17

Unwilling to leave the intimacy of the moment, Sara nevertheless knew it was time to rejoin the event before she was missed. Unwinding herself from the tangled embrace they shared she stepped back, missing the heat of Mitch instantly.

"We need to get back."

"I know." He straightened, grabbing his jacket but not putting it back on. "We can leave early, right?"

She giggled at his cheekily lascivious smirk.

"You haven't even met my parents yet."

"Well lead on Princess. Let's get this done."

Re-entering the ballroom she blinked, struggling to adjust from the dim lighting of the back corridors. Since they'd been gone, the space had swelled with mingling guests, and it took a moment to locate her parents. Finally spotting them, she took Mitch's hand and began navigating the crowd toward them. She'd only taken a few steps when a hand on her arm forced her to stop.

"Sara, how nice to see you again," said Phil, his eyes locked on Mitch. "And you've brought a bodyguard, how nice."

"What?" she glanced between the two men in confusion. "Phil, this is Mitch, my boyfriend. Mitch, this is Phil. We used to date," she added reluctantly.

"Your boyfriend? Jesus Sara, you've gone from dating me

to seeing this gorilla?"

Tensing, she looked to Mitch with wide eyes, afraid of his reaction. Leaning into her ear he whispered. "Relax baby."

Having not riled Mitch, as was no doubt his intention, Phil jerked back into a passing waiter. Without pausing, he grabbed the jug of water from the waiter's tray and sloshed the whole thing over Mitch's white dress shirt. "Oh look, clumsy me," he sneered in mock apology, before stalking away.

Stunned, Sara could only watch his retreating back.

"That was insane, I have no idea why he did that."

"I have a small idea," Mitch grimaced, using the jacket draped over his arm to dry his face.

Sara was distracted from responding when she realized the water had caused his white shirt to cling to the well-defined muscles of his torso, revealing his tattoos. For a purely feminine moment, she couldn't help but revel in his savage beauty, her thighs clenching together in need.

Shaking herself, she realized their spectacle had garnered a small group of onlookers, who were gaping at Mitch. With his hair mussed from her fingers running through it and his heavily inked skin, he looked every inch the uncivilized Viking she adored.

"Well it's not like mum and dad aren't going to find out about the tattoos. You *are* a tattoo artist." Her smile faltered at the grim set of his mouth. "I'm sorry Phil was a jerk. But don't worry about it, it's just water," she reassured.

"I don't give a fuck about that asshole. I just wanted to make a good first impression with your parents. It would have been nice to get to know them before they passed judgement based on my appearance."

"They aren't going to judge you." She hoped he didn't

notice her surreptitiously crossing her fingers. "Come on, let's get a drink from the bar before we see them."

With a curt nod he followed her, her heart sinking at his abrupt change of attitude. She could feel the lengthening space between them, even as their hands clasped and fingers twined. It was nothing a whiskey couldn't fix, right?

Several minutes later Sara had to concede that no, maybe a whiskey – or in Mitch's case, three – couldn't fix it. He'd downed them in quick succession, the bartender giving her side eyes.

Mitch's features had taken on a brittle quality and his mood was descending by the second.

"Maybe we need to sneak back to our secret room," she joked quietly, tugging on his arm to get him to face her, hoping to soften him.

"Now you're afraid for your parents to meet me?"

"You know that's not true," she beseeched.

He rubbed a hand over his eyes, sighing. "You're right, I'm sorry. I'm being a dick. I just don't want to fuck this up," he admitted. "Are you okay here for a moment while I use the restroom?"

"Of course."

His arm brushed against Darla Simmons as he turned to leave, and Sara's eyes narrowed when Darla tittered at her companion. "Goodness. I'm going to need a tetanus shot now."

Sucking in a sharp breath, Sara watched as Mitch's shoulders tensed, before he forged through the crowd. There was no doubt he'd overheard Darla's snide comment.

"Darla Simmons. That was unforgivably rude," she hissed. Darla swung in surprise, her face reddening.

"Oh! Sara darling. It was just a little joke. He's just so, so *uncouth.*"

"The only one lacking manners at the moment is you," Sara retorted. "I'm embarrassed by your lack of decorum, not his."

Darla gaped unattractively and Sara spun on her heel to follow Mitch.

She had a bad feeling in the pit of her stomach, which intensified when she saw the set of Mitch's jaw as he rejoined her. "Are you okay?"

"I'm fine, let's just get his over and done with, okay?"

Sara was disappointed at his behavior, even while she understood it. She desperately wanted her parents to see Mitch the way she did, and she was worried that in his current state of mind that was going to be near impossible.

"Okay, let's go," she said, feigning brightness. Her parents were chatting with Michael Browne, an old family friend and a State MP.

"It's a shame that legislation got passed, but there are ways to get around it," he was saying, breaking off when he spotted Sara.

"Sara my dear child, it's so good to see you." He clasped her in a hug. "You get more beautiful every time I see you."

"Oh stop it Michael." She patted him affectionately on the back. "I haven't seen you in forever."

"And who's this?" his gaze rested on Mitch. "You've got yourself a beau?"

"I don't know what the fuck a beau is, I'm her boyfriend."

Sara winced and jabbed an elbow into Mitch's side.

After a moment of stunned silence, Michael and her father gave an awkward chuckle.

"Well in that case, it's nice to meet you. I'm Stephen, Sara's father." Her dad stepped forward and offered his hand to shake. Mitch stared at it sullenly and remained still.

Sara's cheeks burnt with mortification and she had a brief out of body moment, wondering if this was actually happening.

What the fuck *is he doing?*

"If you'll excuse me, I think I'll go and get another drink," Michael murmured.

With his departure, the full weight of her parent's surprise was evident, their gazes flicking between Sara and Mitch. How ironic to only realise she loved Mitch as he was breaking her heart.

"It's nice to meet you," her mother said, attempting to alleviate the tension. "I'm Teresa. Tell me Mitch, where did you go to school?"

Sara grimaced at the unconscious snobbery.

"Cabramatta High," Mitch replied in a flat voice before she could intervene. Her mother's wince would have been comical if it weren't so damaging.

"Is that not good enough for you?" he challenged.

"Son, if you're going to be seeing my daughter, I expect a little more respect," her father said in a low voice. "And if you can't manage that, then I think it's time you left."

"You're right. It is time I left," Mitch muttered, not meeting her eyes. And before she could utter a word of protest, he'd gone.

———

Slugging whiskey straight from the bottle Mitch swallowed the burning liquid, before letting his head fall back against Simon's sofa.

"I'm all for drinking your pain away, but at least tell me what happened," Simon said, slouching down beside him. "And slow up. Why don't you switch to beer?"

"Fuck your beer," Mitch slurred.

"Well that's three words more than I've gotten since you arrived and helped yourself to my liquor cabinet," sighed Simon. "Come on man, you rock up at 11 o'clock on a Saturday night – you're lucky I was in, by the way – and proceed to drink enough to sink a bloody ship. What happened?"

"I fucked up. I fucked everything. Everything is fucked."

"That's a lot of fucks man."

The bottle slipped from his loose grasp, and Simon caught it before it hit the floor. Mitch's only reaction was to close his eyes.

"Okay. That's enough of that. Sleep it off on my couch, and we'll talk in the morning, okay?"

"Fuck you."

"Fuck you too brother."

Morning light stabbed at the back of his skull, even with his forearm thrown over his eyes. His gut was roiling and his mouth was dry. Hangover from hell.

"You deserve to feel like shit, you know that, right?" It was Maggie, leaning over him and pressing a damp washcloth to his forehead. "And before you swear at me, Ruby is in the next room watching television, so watch your mouth."

Rolling to his side on the couch he'd apparently slept on, he opened bleary eyes at his sister.

"I ruined everything," he admitted, not even trying to stem the despair that tainted his words. "She's never going to want to see me again."

"Who, Sara?"

He nodded mutely.

"Water, paracetamol and coffee," announced Simon, entering the room. "You, my friend, are going to be hungover for a week."

Sitting up to accept the water and drugs, Mitch winced. His whole body throbbed in pain. Which was nothing compared to the ache in his chest.

"I thought I could be in her world. I thought we could make it work. But I saw the way they looked at me. And that's nothing to how she'd look at me once she learned the truth. And that would kill me." He shut his eyes tight, trying to block the memory. "So I was the shittiest jerk I could be. I was an asshole of epic proportions. And she's never going to want to see me again. But at least I won't ever have to see her look at me like she would if she knew."

Simon and Maggie exchanged looks.

Maggie's voice was gentle; "You mean about Stu." It was a statement, not a question. "You didn't tell her that to protect me, to keep me safe, you smacked around the guy that tried to rape me? That some stupid hanger-on friend didn't know when to stop and beat him to death? Because that wasn't on you Mitch. It wasn't your fault."

"I didn't know that Leon had been harassing you at school. I should have protected you better."

"You didn't know because I didn't *tell you* Mitch. I didn't want to put more worry on you because I thought I could handle it myself."

"I will *always* worry about you little sister," he said gruffly, pulling her into a tight hug. After a moment he sighed. "Wendel was convicted and didn't rat on either of us. He didn't say a word."

"That was his choice, Mitch. We didn't ask him to do that. And even if he had, we assaulted the guy – we didn't kill him," said Simon firmly.

"No, but I was the reason Wendel did."

"That's like saying it was my fault because the guy tried to rape me," Maggie retorted angrily. "And I don't even know why this is suddenly an issue."

"Because Jennifer's new boyfriend is Wendel. And he's only screwing with her to get to me. He wants me to push drugs for him through the studio."

"What the fuck man! Why are you only just telling us this now?" exclaimed Simon, jumping to his feet and pacing the room. "Does Jennifer know?"

"I haven't told her all of it. I just warned her to stay away, and she told me to fuck off."

"What do you mean you didn't tell her all of it? You dickhead. She needs to know this!" cried Maggie, digging through her handbag to find her phone and rapidly texting Jennifer.

"Man, go and shower while we wait for Jenn," suggested Simon. "I'm going to get drunk just smelling you. I've left some of my clothes in the bathroom for you to change into."

Mitch felt marginally better when he emerged from the bathroom 20 minutes later. That was, until he saw Jennifer.

"You are such a jerk, you know that?" Jennifer yelled.

"You let me keep seeing Stu when he hadn't told me he'd been in jail *and* he was trying to blackmail you! For fuck's sake Mitch, I thought you were smarter than that." She quietened, sitting back down at the kitchen table. "I thought I meant more to you than that."

He felt that like a kick in the guts.

"Jenn, I'm so sorry. I just didn't know what to do. Wendel is fucking unbalanced, and I didn't want to stir him up – I didn't know what he'd do. I was just hoping that if you broke things off with him, and I ignored him, that he'd go away."

"He's not going anywhere Mitch. I did break up with him, yesterday. He was getting all creepy asking questions about you and Sara, and I guess I realized the vibe I was getting from him was less hot bad boy and more deranged psycho."

"What do you mean he's not going anywhere?" worried Maggie.

"He laughed at me and said I'd change my mind, and that I wouldn't be able to help seeing him because he and Mitch were business partners now."

Mitch stood, slamming his fist onto the table and making Jennifer jump.

"Sorry! Sorry. I just feel fucking trapped. What if he does something to you or Sara or Maggie if I don't play along? I don't know what to do."

"We go to the police, you big dumbass," said Maggie, as if it were the simplest thing in the world. "He can't hurt anyone if he's back behind bars."

Sitting heavily, Mitch dropped his head into his hands. Maggie was right. What did it matter if he also ended up behind bars for his part in the murder? He just needed to make sure that Wendel couldn't touch his loved ones.

"Okay, let's do it."

Leaving the police station several hours later with Maggie by his side, Mitch felt lighter than he had in years. The statute of limitation meant he was in the clear for his assault on Leon, with the police much more interested in Wendel's attempted blackmail.

"Turns out that removing the threat of doing hard time is a great hangover cure," he grinned.

"You were never going to jail, you goose. I'm just sorry I didn't realise how much blame you were carrying all these years." She linked her arm through his. "That Drug Squad Detective sure was interested in Stu."

"As long as they pick him up soon, I don't care what kind of hard on the detective has for him. Until we get a call saying he's back in custody, I want everyone to be extra careful, okay?"

"His parole officer seemed pretty confident they'd have him in a matter of hours," Maggie comforted. "Now you just have to sort things out with Sara."

Mitch's resolve hardened. If we could face the police, he could damn well man up and face Sara's parents to apologise. And hope like hell they'd be willing to give him a second chance.

Dropping Maggie off back at his apartment, he watched her until she'd entered the building before heading for the Queen Street deli Sara was always mooning over. After dropping an obscene amount of money on cheese, along with a bouquet of flowers from the florist next door, he found a park easily enough on Ocean Road and sat in his car staring at Sara's childhood home. For the first time, the difference between their upbringings didn't leave him feeling cold. Sure, his past was unsavory, but today he'd moved past it. Walking out of the police station, he finally let himself believe that the man he was today could be worthy of the woman he loved.

With his arms full and wearing Simon's borrowed clothes he walked up the hedged walkway to the front door and resolutely rang the doorbell, hearing it discreetly chiming within.

"Oh, my." Sara's mother opened the door and gasped at the sight of him. Taking a step back she called for her husband, never taking her silver grey eyes off him.

"You've got a lot of nerve son, I'll give you that," Stephen stated, opening the door wider so he and Teresa could stand shoulder to shoulder.

Mitch steeled himself, ready to face the judgement and condemnation he deserved.

"I'm sorry. Last night I was unforgivably rude. I sabotaged myself because I thought I couldn't be good enough for your daughter. But I can. I can be good enough for her. And I'm going to spend the rest of my life proving that to you, and to her." He handed his peace offerings to Sara's mother. "I really am so sorry for my behavior." He took his first real deep breath in what felt like forever.

Teresa held the gifts gingerly, away from her body, and made no response.

"It's going to take more than flowers to prove your worthiness," Stephen stated flatly, his arms crossed. "But it's a start," he acquiesced.

CHAPTER 18

Sara considered not answering the knock at her apartment door. She was barefoot in black leggings and an oversize sweatshirt, her hair a tumbling mess and her face blotchy from crying.

It didn't matter who was on the other side of the door – she didn't want to see them. Her heart was broken into a thousand different pieces, and the unexpected grief was a jagged blade that was cutting her up inside.

The knock sounded again, at the same time her phone received a text message.

Jennifer: I know Mitch was an asshole, but he had his reasons. Hear him out, okay?

Dropping her phone onto the coffee table she sighed and opened the door.

It wasn't Mitch.

Instinctively she started to close it, but the man held his hands open in supplication. "I'm Stu, Jennifer's boyfriend," he said.

"What are you doing here? Did she send you?" she asked in confusion. The guy was leanly muscled and tall, with close cropped hair and amateur-looking tattoos that were a stark contrast to Mitch's beautiful ink.

What kind of person has DIY tattoos?

"I don't understand why you're here?"

"Yeah, Jenn sent me. She needs me to give you a lift to Mitch."

"Well that's too bad. I don't want to see Mitch."

"Ah come on doll, I'm just trying to do my missus a favour."

"Don't call me doll," she responded automatically. "And seriously, I don't want to go anywhere." She started to close the door again, but his booted foot wedged it open.

"What are you doing?" Alarm spiked through her. "I told you, I don't want to go anywhere. It was nice to meet you, but you need to leave now."

"You really are a high society bitch, aren't you? Telling me it was nice to meet me even though I'm about to tie you up."

His face was still open and friendly, and it took a moment for his words to penetrate.

"You what?!" Frantically she used both hands to push against the door, but he easily shoved it open, slamming it shut behind him as she stumbled backwards.

She stared at him in shock. This was Jennifer's *boyfriend*??

"You need to go. Whatever this is, I want it to stop."

"That's cute. You want it to stop. I bet you're used to getting what you want," he grinned, his affable manner at total odds to his words and actions.

Spinning, Sara dashed to the coffee table and grabbed at her phone, her hands shaking as she tried to unlock it.

Stu strolled over and plucked it from her hands. "Oh I don't think so."

She watched in horror as he dropped it into a glass of water on the kitchen counter. "We're going to have some fun, you and I. Because Mitch needs to learn to pay his debts and play by the rules. My rules."

Backing away from him, Sara ran for the bathroom and slammed the door shut, leaning back against it with all her strength. Why the fuck didn't she have a lock on this door? Adrenaline kept her upright as she locked her knees together and braced, ready for the push she knew would come from the other side. She knew implacably that right now, with her life in danger, the only person she wanted was Mitch.

She jerked when Stu's calm voice came through the door, obviously just inches away.

"See what you need to understand Sara, is that if you don't cooperate with me, then I'll have to go and visit with Maggie, and that little girl of hers. Ruby. She's a cute little poppet, isn't she. What does Mitch call her? Apple?"

Tears sliding silently down her cheeks, Sara's breath caught. The idea of this creep anywhere near Ruby made her want to throw up.

"All you have to do is come out here and talk to me. I need you to make Mitch understand that I'm in control here, and he needs to start falling into line."

"Are you going to tie me up?" she asked in a shaky voice.

"It's nothing personal doll, but I can't have you trying to stab me with a kitchen knife, now can I?"

"But you won't hurt me?"

If she could somehow keep him talking and get to her laptop, she could send a message for help. But trapped in the bathroom, she couldn't do a damn thing. There was no point in trying to wait him out, she already knew there was no one coming to rescue her and besides, he could easily push his way in if he wanted to.

The best she could do was pretend compliance and wait for the opportunity to either make a run for it, or send an SOS.

"Of course I won't hurt you. What do you think I am, a monster?"

"That's exactly what I think you are," she muttered to herself, gently easing her weight from the door and rummaging through the bathroom drawer to find the only weapon she could think of – a pair of nail scissors. Having them in the pocket of her sweatshirt didn't make her feel any better, they just reinforced how out of her depth she was.

Slipping from the bathroom she warily watched Stu, who was casually leaning against the wall opposite her.

"Okay, now we're getting somewhere," he said approvingly. "Good girl. Turn around and put your hands behind your back."

Obediently she did so, spying her set of golf clubs in the corner to her right.

Thank you for the golf lessons Daddy.

Lunging, she grasped at a nine iron and twirled, panting heavily.

"You aren't going to tie me up, and you are *not* going to use me against Mitch."

"Feisty little bitch, aren't you? I think there's a lot he'd do for you."

"You need to leave. Right now!" Sara raised the golf club and steeled herself. She wasn't going to back down. She could, and would, swing this club to defend herself.

"Get the fuck OUT!" she screamed.

It was unnerving how calm Stu was in the face of her fury.

"Or what? You going to take a swing at me?"

Righteous adrenalin had dissolved the lump of fear in her

throat and an instinct for survival raged hot in her chest.

There was no time to think. She ran at him and swung hard, aiming for his head.

It was a mistake.

He was taller than her and aiming for that height put her off balance. In an instant he had side-stepped and rushed her, his shoulder checking her and forcing her to stumble back.

"Put the fucking golf club down," he growled.

"No." Her white-knuckled grip didn't falter.

Until he pulled a hand gun from his back pocket.

"Put the fucking golf club down," he repeated.

Dizzy with shock at the sight of the weapon, she dropped her arms, nausea rolling in her stomach.

Approaching her confidently, Stu removed the golf club from her slack fingers and turned her. She felt hard plastic ties circling her wrists restraining them together. Breathing through the panic she reminded herself he hadn't tied her feet. She could run if she got the chance.

"See, that wasn't so bad, was it?" he crooned, his hands on her shoulders turning her to face him. She flinched at the contact. "Now I just need to get a quick photo of you to send to your boyfriend, and then we're going on a little ride together."

"What? No! You can't kidnap me!"

"Doll, I have you tied up and this nice gun. I can do whatever I want to you," he tutted at her, stepping back to get more of her in the frame as he snapped a photo on his phone. "Mitch just needs a little incentive to get the ball rolling and as long as he does what he's told, no one is going to get hurt," he responded, tapping at his phone.

"What do you want him to do? Why does he owe you?"

This whole crazy mess was so confusing.

"Mitch and I killed a kid years ago, and I went to prison for it and didn't rat on him. So he owes me, plain and simple. I need to make some cash, and I have a contact with an excellent drug supply. Mitch is going to move the product for me through his business."

Sara's head spun. Mitch had killed someone? A kid?

"I don't believe you."

"Doesn't matter to me if you do or not," he shrugged. "I'm parked just out the front, and you're going to walk nice and quiet with me out to the car and get inside." Removing his jacket he placed it over her shoulders, effectively concealing the fact her hands were bound. "And before you get any grand plans to yell for help, know that my gun is held against your back." To emphasize the point, she felt a dull prod in her spine. "So let's go doll, nice and quiet."

"I don't have any shoes on," she stalled.

"You don't need them," he soothed. She shuddered. This guy was creepy as *fuck*. And gun or no gun, if there was someone on the street she was taking the chance to yell for help. She didn't want to believe he'd risk getting caught by shooting her.

"What's your way out of this?" she asked. "Even if Mitch agrees to sell the drugs for you, what's to stop him from telling the police? What's to stop *me* from going to the police when you let me go?"

"Who says I'm going to let you go?" he responded mildly. "Just kidding," he laughed at her wild eyes. "We're all going to be friends, you'll see. Although I was a little hurt that you didn't keep the bear I gave you."

"What? What bear?" This guy was insane.

"The one I delivered to your office. It was a token of friendship. I was bummed when I found it in the dumpster out the back of your office building."

Nausea rose, hot and metallic.

"You took that nail polish from my desk and gave it to Jenn," she whispered, the obviousness a slap in the face.

"Time to go now," he smiled, ignoring her.

Walking at her shoulder he steered her into the elevator and out the front entrance to her building, all without seeing another person.

Where is *everyone?*

He led her to a white sedan and gestured to the passenger seat.

"Remember, nice and quiet."

From the corner of her eye, Sara saw an elderly man walking a dog round the corner about 200 meters from her. She opened her mouth to scream but Stu was faster. There was a sharp crack as the butt of the gun slammed into the back of her head, and then nothing.

———

Frustration rode Mitch hard. Sara wasn't picking up her phone and a creeping dread was rising in his gut. He couldn't explain it, but he knew it wasn't just Sara ignoring him.

Something was wrong.

At the alert of a text message he snatched at his phone, desperate for it to be her, only to howl in anguish when he saw the photo Wendel had sent. Slamming his fists onto the steering wheel of his stationary car, another cry ripped from his throat.

The sight of Sara, desperately frightened and with her hands bound, had his mind blanking in fury and fear.

It took several tries to send the text, his hands were shaking so badly his fingers fumbled over the screen of his smartphone. Parked on the side of the street, with traffic streaming around him and pedestrians strolling along the pavement, the confine of his vehicle was suddenly an airless, soundless vacuum.

Heart hammering, he gulped in air. Fumbling in his wallet he pulled out the business card the drug squad detective had given him and punched the numbers into his phone, anxiety ratcheting up a notch at every unanswered ring.

"Detective Carlson."

"It's Mitch Smith, I just saw you this morning. Stu Wendel has my girlfriend and I need your help."

"How do you know he has your girlfriend?"

"He just sent me a photo of her, in her home I think, and her hands are tied behind her back and she looks fucking scared," his voice broke.

The detective snapped into action. "What's your girlfriend's full name and address? We'll send a squad straight there, and I'm putting an immediate alert out on his vehicle."

Mitch answered rapidly, already putting his car into drive and accelerating into the traffic.

"Okay. I need you to call me the moment Stu makes

contact again, do you understand?"

"Yes. I'm on my way to her apartment now."

"I'll meet you there. But do not, under any circumstances, approach her apartment. You've got to let us do our job."

It took an agonizing ten minutes to reach Sara's apartment building, which had several police vehicles parked outside, lights flashing. Spotting Carlson he ran to him, chest rising and falling as though he'd run a marathon.

"Is she in there?"

"No. I want you to put your phone on speaker and call Stu. We need to know what he's trying to accomplish here."

"He thinks he can use Sara as leverage to blackmail me into helping him. He's fucking deranged to think it's going to work."

"His parole office did mention there were some mental issues," Carlson admitted. "Try and call him, we'll see if he's willing to talk."

Before he could do so, an officer ran to them with a crackling radio.

"The vehicle has been spotted, and two units are in pursuit. It's heading north on Anzac Parade."

"Okay everyone, let's mobilize!" ordered Carlson. "Mitch, you're with me."

Sirens joining the flashing lights, the police tore through the hastily parting traffic. Mitch's fists were bloodless he was clenching them so tight. If anything happened to Sara he wouldn't be able to live with himself.

In just minutes the police radio broke the tense silence. "Suspect has been apprehended, with no casualties."

Relief crashed through him as Carlson turned to him and grinned. Picking up the radio handset he spoke into it. "And

Sara Morrison? Is she safe?"

"Could have a slight concussion and in shock, but otherwise fine," the voice came back. "The ambulance is taking her direct to Prince of Wales Hospital."

"I'll drop you there and then head back to the station," said Carlson. "I'm looking forward to having a chat with Stu Wendel. I think he's the link to some big players I've been gunning for." This time, his grin was slightly feral.

"I'll need both you and Sara to come to the station to give a statement, but you can wait until tomorrow for that."

Carlson let him out at the doors to the emergency department and after asking anxiously at the front desk he was directed to a small, curtained-off cubicle. Hesitating, he stood outside the curtain trying to control his breathing. The fear for Sara's safety had been replaced by the fear she wouldn't want to see him, and he didn't know if he could handle that.

Knowing she'd been put in danger because of his tainted past and her relationship with him was a gnawing, festering wound inside his chest. The thought that she wouldn't be able to forgive him was almost more than he could bear.

"Sara?" he called softly, slowly pulling aside the curtain enough to step through.

His heart stopped.

She looked so tiny, wearing a hospital gown and propped up in the bed. She opened those big grey eyes of hers and, seeing him, they instantly filled with tears that spilled over and down her pale cheeks.

"Oh god, Princess," the groan was wrenched from him and he strode to her side, terrified she would shrink back from him but unable to keep his distance. "I'm sorry. I'm so, so sorry."

When she lifted her arms towards him, it was balm to his soul. The smell of antiseptic, the bustling beyond the curtain, all receded. He dropped to the bed and dragged her into his arms, feeling the burn of tears at the back of his throat when her arms wound around his neck and she clung tight.

"Are you hurt baby? Are you okay? Oh God, I'm so sorry," he murmured into her hair, his hands running up and down her back, drawing her closer against him.

They stayed that way, slightly rocking and with him crooning to her, for what could have been an hour, or mere moments. Time had no meaning now that Sara was safe back in his arms.

When she pulled back slightly he let her, wanting to see her face when he confessed. When he showed her who he truly was.

"He said," she paused, glancing away and then resolutely locking eyes with him. "He said that you killed someone. And that he took the blame for it." She raised a hand to trail her fingers down his stubbled cheek. "I don't want to believe that Mitch. Tell me it's not true."

"It's true, and it's not," he replied slowly. "I think I've only just absolved myself of the blame – for a long time I thought it *was* my fault."

"But it wasn't?" She was so hopeful and sweet and trusting and he ached to not have to share this story with her.

"When I was 17, and Maggie was 15, a classmate of hers followed her home, broke into the house and tried to," he stopped to swallow. "He tried to rape her. He assaulted her and if I hadn't come home when I did, he would have violated her. She was sobbing in my arms and I needed to protect her.

I wanted that kid to hurt in the worst way, and I needed him to never come near her again. So Simon and I tracked him down and we, we gave him a beating. A beating that I would have gone to juvvie for. And Wendel was there and he just kept smacking into the kid, even when we pulled back and I told him to stop. He had some sort of crazed blood lust thing happening and we couldn't reason with him. So we ran.

We ran, and Wendel got caught with a dead body and when he was arrested he didn't say anything about me or Simon. He took all the blame, and went away for a long time," he paused, closing his eyes and sighing. "And now he's out, and he hooked up with Jennifer to try and get to me, because he thinks I owe him. And when I said no, he took you. God, I am *so* sorry baby."

"So it's true, and it's not," she repeated his words, pondering them. "Okay. As much as I want to know why you didn't tell me, I guess, well – I guess I know. You were worried about how I'd react. And you were right to worry, because I was so consumed with what other people thought that I wouldn't have let myself fall in love with you."

The hairs on his arms electrified.

"You love me?"

"Yes I love you, you big jerk."

"Enough to forgive me?"

"If you promise to stop being such a jerk," she smiled. "And can you kiss me already?"

"Tell me you love me again."

"I love you."

She started at the size of the grin stretching his face. "You like that idea, huh?"

"I like it a lot Princess."

Bracing his hands against the mattress on either side of her, he leant forward and caught her lips in the barest hint of kiss, softly brushing against her softness. When she opened for him he pressed deeper, needing to imprint her on his soul. Her breath was his breath and he couldn't get close enough. His lips slanted over hers, his tongue licked and caressed. She clutched at the nape of his neck and her soft mewling drove him on, one of his hands coming up to cup her jaw, angling her for better access. It was more than a kiss. It was absolution. And in it, he found peace.

CHAPTER 19

It had been two weeks since "the incident", as her parents referred to it, and in that time she and Mitch had fallen into the rhythm of their relationship. They'd had a quiet dinner with her parents, who were cautiously approving of Mitch, and he spent most nights in her bed.

He was an insatiable itch under her skin that no amount of orgasms, or sunrise walks on the beach, or breakfast smoothies or lunchtime quickies, seemed to be able to cure. The more time she spent with him, the deeper she fell. And she'd already been deep.

Now, with sand between her toes and the sun warm on her skin, she'd never been happier. Running hands through her newly lilac-streaked platinum hair she sighed in contentment.

Hunting away a questing seagull, Mitch reached down to pull her up from her beach towel, his hands squeezing her ass as he pretended to dust the sand away.

"Time to go Princess. You have an appointment to get to," he instructed, setting her away and gathering up their towels.

Anticipation fizzed through her. Holding hands, they made their way up to the Bondi promenade, Sara pinching Mitch's side every time a woman took a second look at his shirtless torso.

"Would you stop that?" Tickling her, he hauled her over his shoulder in a fireman's hold, entering Ink Inc.

"You too are so cute you make me want to barf," Jennifer

commented dryly. "And you're tracking sand all over my clean floor."

"Hi Jenn!" Sara called, upside down.

"We'll be in my room. Don't disturb us," Mitch directed.

"There is not a chance of that happening," Jennifer responded.

As he set her down on the floor to close and lock the door, Sara riffled through her bag to replace her sunglasses with her glasses. Absently, she realized that since being with Mitch, she'd become less preoccupied with her appearance, more often than not forgoing her contacts for glasses. And taking *much* less time to fuss with her makeup.

There was something to be said about the love of a good man making you more comfortable in your own skin.

"Fuck I love when you wear these," Mitch said huskily, ducking his head to kiss her, their tongues tangling lazily. His hands rose under her sundress to cup her ass, pulling her snug against his erection. Thumbs sliding beneath the edge of her bikini bottoms he squeezed and molded, deepening the kiss.

Pulling away he placed her gently back onto her feet. "Jesus, I can't get enough of you," he growled.

"I can feel that," she smirked, palming the impressive bulge in his surf shorts. "I hope you're professional enough to be able to tattoo even with a hard on."

"Oh I'm professional all right," he said, snapping on black latex gloves and rolling a trolley with his equipment over to the reclining chair.

"Do you always tattoo women behind locked doors and without wearing a shirt?" she asked coyly, slowly pulling the sundress over her head and reveling in his expression as he took in her bikini-clad body.

"If you want my full concentration, you'd better leave the dress on," he admitted hoarsely.

"But maybe I need it off. You still don't know where I want the tattoo," she reminded him, starting to tug at the tie behind her back that kept the tiny triangles of her swimwear together.

Mitch growled again, picking her up bodily and depositing her on the tattoo chair. "Leave the bikini on, Princess. Otherwise I'll be balls deep in that beautiful pussy of yours in 2.3 seconds. I've waited a long time for the chance to tattoo this skin. Let me enjoy the moment."

Smiling languorously, Sara stretched out on the chair, one pointed toe traversing the contours of her other calf seductively.

"I'm okay with fucking first," she purred. Her pulse was thumping hard, down low, and she ached to feel him buried inside her.

"You're going to get spanked in a moment," he threatened.

Her eyes lit up. "Really? Because I think I might like that."

"Have mercy woman," he groaned. "Don't you want to see the design?"

They had decided Mitch would design a tattoo for her, and she would choose the size and placement. She had complete confidence in whatever he'd drawn, but she still didn't know what it was. And she was as curious as hell.

Sitting forward eagerly she abandoned her seduction attempt. For now.

"Okay, you have my attention."

"First, I want to show you something I had Simon do yesterday."

She blinked slowly.

"Bringing Simon into this is kind of killing the mood."

He grinned wolfishly and removed his watch, which she noticed he was wearing on the right wrist instead of the left. Extending his arm – wrist up – she gasped.

"It's beautiful."

"It's a Norse crown. For a Viking queen. For you, Sara."

Speechless, she stroked her thumb across the black inkwork, tears pricking her eyes.

Moving to a drawer, Mitch withdrew a sheet of paper and brought it to her. "And this is a dragonfly, which represents strength. Because you are strong, and delicate and beautiful." The drawing was intricate and feminine, capturing the elusiveness of the delicately winged creature.

"Oh god, I love it," she exclaimed, taking the piece of paper and studying it intently. "It's beautiful. Beyond beautiful. It's perfect."

"Good." The timbre of his voice had roughened, and Sara realized how much he'd needed her to approve his work.

"I want it on me, now," she demanded.

"Where?"

She'd been thinking on her ankle, or maybe her side, just below her boob. But having seen the design she knew she wanted to be able to see it constantly. "On the inside of my wrist, where yours is."

"Discreet," he mused. "You can always cover it with your watch."

"No. I want it on my right wrist. I don't want to cover it up."

Pleased, he nodded.

"Okay baby, let's do this."

Belatedly, she felt a prickle of trepidation. "It's going to hurt, isn't it?"

"A little. Not much."

Taking her wrist in his big hand he leant over her, and then the buzzing of his tattoo gun was vibrating against her wrist. It was a hot, stinging sensation as the needle dragged over the skin, but not enough to make her flinch. She held steady at the manageable discomfort and stared at Mitch's bent head, his self-assured concentration an aphrodisiac all on its own.

The buzz of the gun stopped and Sara realised it was finished.

"That was quick."

"It's only small babe. Don't look yet, let me clean it first."

He swiped an alcohol wipe over the area and then raised her wrist to his lips, kissing it gently. "I love that you have my ink on your skin."

Letting go, he allowed her to study the fresh tattoo, the skin around it pink.

"I love it," she said, throwing herself into his arms.

He laughed, peeling off his gloves and maneuvering her until she was straddling his lap, his thick cock positioned perfectly for her to grind down on.

"You make me so unbelievably happy."

"Right back at you Princess."

"Can we fuck now?"

He laughed harder.

———

Mitch still delighted in hearing Sara curse. Especially when she was wearing those sexy-as-fuck glasses. In fact, everything about her delighted him. He was a ray of fucking sunshine now that she was his.

Gathering her in his arms he stood, walking over to the spare tattoo chair that had already been lowered to a horizontal position. "Yes Princess, we can fuck," he promised.

Sliding her down his body to stand on unsteady legs, he drew a deliberate finger from her chin, down the slender column of her throat and into her luscious cleavage. She gasped, but didn't move.

"I want you naked Princess," he instructed, stepping back slightly.

With unsteady fingers she loosened the knots holding her bikini in place and the scraps of fabric fell to the floor leaving her bare for him. All that succulent skin and sweet, soft curves that he wanted to sink his teeth into.

He swallowed, willing his control to stay the course.

"Now turn around, brace your elbows on the chair and spread your legs for me."

When she complied, glancing back over her shoulder at him with fervent eyes, he came close to losing it. She was everything he never knew he wanted, and now couldn't live without.

Crowding behind her he pressed himself against her pert, upturned ass, leaning over and kissing her impatiently. One hand braced his weight on the chair near her head while the other palmed her tits hungrily.

She arched her back on a breathy moan when he trailed his mouth down her neck, sucking hard enough to leave marks. Kissing down the sweet curve of her spine he knelt behind her, breathing in her arousal and feeling it spike his blood.

His bracing hand left the bed and settled on her lower

back, pushing down so she instinctively raised her ass higher, giving him the access he craved. Bringing his head between her thighs he traced a finger over her tight rosebud and spread her pussy, delving deep with his tongue.

Her legs shook and her thighs tensed before opening wider. Her muffled moan told him she was biting down on something in a bid to be discreet.

He would never tire of the taste of her. Of the sounds she made while he drove her crazy with his tongue, flicking and licking and plunging.

"Fuck, Mitch! I want to come," she begged.

Edging her to the cusp of orgasm and pulling back had become his favourite pastime, knowing the intensity when he finally allowed her release would devastate her in the most beautiful way.

Getting to his feet he shed his sneakers and shorts, loving the sight of his big, naked body standing before her small, needy one. Her expression was blissful, cheek turned to the side and hair a wild tangle around her head.

Rolling on a condom, his cock slapped against his lower abdomen, his balls drawing tight. Her mouth opened on a silent 'o' of pleasure as he gripped her hips and slammed his cock home, filling her tightness with his thick length.

Twining one hand in her hair, he rocked his hips, seating himself as fully inside her as he could. She began mindlessly chanting his name, pushing back and urging him deeper. Faster.

Denying her, he slowed to an unhurried pulse – easing in and out with agonizing leisure, sweat forming on his brow at the forced restraint.

When she pleaded for more, he reached around and

pinched gently at a nipple, rolling it between his fingers. But when she tried to reach between their bodies to touch herself Mitch relented.

"Okay baby, okay," he soothed, withdrawing to pick her up and lie her back on the chair. Kneeling upright on the chair above her he hooked his hands around her ankles and brought both of them to rest on one of his shoulders, flexing his hips to drive deep into her.

"Oh fuck! That's so good," she cried, biting down on her lower lip.

Wrapping an arm around her legs, he placed the other on her stomach to hold her steady as he thrust in firm, rocking movements. Knowing he couldn't last much longer he leaned back, altering the angle of penetration and was instantly rewarded with her clenching convulsively around his cock, his name shouted from her lips. His balls drawing tight he allowed his own orgasm to claim him, head falling back as he ferociously pumped his release before falling to cover her.

Chest to chest, soul to soul, they came down from their shared high, heart beats slowly returning to normal. Bracing himself on his elbows so he wouldn't crush her, he admired the goddess spread out before him, cheeks flushed and eyes bright. His chest expanded with the strength of love for this woman, who had invaded and conquered his heart.

"Mad chemistry," she mumbled drowsily.

"Mad chemistry," he agreed, and kissed her long and true.

THE END

ACKNOWLEDGEMENTS

I would like to thank the authors who attended the 2019 Australian Romance Readers Association awards evening – being amongst them inspired me to finish this manuscript (I'd stalled for over 12 months after the first sex scene). The support and encouragement of the romance community is really fucking awesome.

And to Sarah Proulx Calfee from Three Little Words Editing, who *gets* me. She added coherency, polish and so. much. awesomeness. to this book. Thank you x

ARE YOU READY FOR
SOPHIE'S STORY?

ANYTHING BUT *Love*

When Sophie's ex-fiancé pulls a disappearing act and Sydney's underworld come knocking, she has no choice but to escape to the outback farm of her ex's brother. Thrown headlong into farming life, Sophie struggles to find her feet… and deny the sizzling attraction to a man she shouldn't want.

Robert is looking for love, but city girl Sophie is not what he wants. Or needs. They're from two different worlds and with his brother placing the family farm in financial jeopardy he can't trust her. Besides, as his brother's ex, she's off-limits. He certainly doesn't expect to be captivated by his brother's girl and, after a night with her, he's not sure he'll be able to let her go.

They promise each other their sexy affair can be anything but love. But amidst the aching beauty of the Australian outback it becomes hard to resist the chance of a once-in-a-lifetime love…

Read on for the first chapter of *Anything But Love*…

CHAPTER 1

The increasingly loud banging on the front door had Sophie frozen. She'd been washing her favourite lace lingerie in the bathroom sink – because the washing machine had died last week – and now she stood, hand dripping on the tiles, her heart beating double time in her chest.

Right. Deep breath.

This couldn't be worse than the recent visit from her real estate agent, who had to personally deliver an eviction notice because she'd been refusing to acknowledge his emails. That had been particularly mortifying and, in the last couple of months, the mortifying moments had been stacking up.

For the tenth time that morning, she cursed her ex-fiancé. When she'd finally called off the engagement and left him, the charisma and bravado he'd been using to financially prop them up had crumbled, and the house of cards they had inhabited had rapidly fallen.

Six months later, the damn man had pulled a disappearing act, taking with him the last of the funds from their joint bank account. Most days, Sophie couldn't determine which emotion was stronger – anger or frustration. Unless you counted her willful blindness to the situation, none of this outcome was her doing, and she was struggling to make sense of her new reality.

"Damien where are you? You'd better make an appearance bloody soon," she muttered under her breath as she wiped her hands on her jeans and headed for the door, which was now rattling on its hinges under the onslaught of fist from the other side.

The sight that greeted her beyond the door's safety chain instantly caused her to take a step backwards, before rushing forward to slam it again. Too late, her guest thrust a large booted foot in the doorway and shouldered it open wide, snapping the so-called safety chain with ease.

"You must be Damien's missus," he stated, his eyes assessing and his mouth a mean line. "Thought I'd better pay you a visit, seeing as he's MIA and darlin', you better know he owes the big boss a lot of cash."

Sophie put a hand to her mouth to quell rising hysteria. Her visitor's eye glinted, his too-thin lips curling in a predatory grin.

She couldn't believe this was now her life. She was a university-educated 26-year old, with a coveted role on the graphic design team of a prestigious women's magazine. She was often in the social pages of Sydney's newspapers, especially after Damien had cemented their It-Couple status by proposing with a seriously large diamond.

Until Damien's gambling had gotten out of control, Sophie had enjoyed a standing appointment for a weekly wash and blow dry of her luxurious honey blonde locks, her nails were always impeccable and the staff at high-end boutique Belinda in Paddington knew her by name.

Life had turned from swanky to skanky with frightening speed and Sophie was way out of her depth.

"He's not here," she stuttered, taking another step back. "And we've broken up – we're not together anymore. Please, just give me your number and I'll pass it on to him."

"Darlin', he already has my number. And he's all out of

chances. He's racked up $420,000 and I'm here to collect."

He reached out a meaty finger and ran it down Sophie's cheek; "I'm pretty sure we can come to some sort of arrangement."

"Like fuck you can," came an angry growl as a large hand clamped down on the intruder's shoulder from behind. Sophie gasped and ran to dodge behind an armchair as shouts and expletives from both males burst forth.

Holy shit.

Sophie was so panicked it took her several moments to realise her rescuer was Robert, Damien's older brother.

What was he doing in Sydney?

He ran the family farm in the middle of god knows where. Sophie had never even met the guy and only recognised him from seeing a few old photos.

Regardless of her non-existent relationship with Robert, he was holding his own against the brutish thug, with both men trading blows equally. Sophie's heart lodged in her throat at the unleashed violence but with adrenaline surging she snatched up the table lamp beside her, coming around the armchair with it held high.

Clutching the heavy lamp base in sweaty hands she flicked her eyes back and forth between the men, waiting for an opportunity to strike, wondering if she had the guts to make it count.

Robert was easily six foot, his broad shoulders were bunched with hard muscle and he obviously knew enough about street fighting. Before Sophie could act, he had knocked the other man to the ground and shoved his cowboy-booted foot against the throat of the fallen man.

"I don't know what the hell you're doing here, but don't

think for a moment you're coming anywhere near her again."

———

Robert's fists remained clenched as he glared down uncompromisingly. He ground his foot down a little harder. "Do. You. Understand?"

The haze of fury that had descended when he'd arrived to find the thug at Sophie's door began to recede. He rolled his shoulders back to ease some tension, but didn't break eye contact. The idea of Sophie in danger was a physical pain, and he redirected it to power the thick muscles of his legs.

The thug grunted and started to thrash his legs, signaling he wasn't getting enough air. With reluctance, Robert removed his foot but stood threateningly, positioning himself between Sophie – who was watching wide-eyed and shaking – and the downed man.

"Get out. And don't ever come back."

The thug was bleeding from the nose and mouth, and getting to all fours he spat a string of bloody saliva onto the carpet. Stumbling to his feet he leered at Sophie, "I'll be seeing you later darlin', and I can't wait to get to know you better."

Fighting to restrain his anger, Robert grabbed the back of the man's shirt and shoved him through the door, firmly closing it behind him. Slowly, he turned to face his brother's fiancé. Now was *not* the time to wonder why he'd been so worked up over a woman he'd never met before. Hell, worked up didn't really describe the blind murderous rage he'd felt, but again, that was something he didn't need to concentrate on right now.

"What the hell was that?" He sounded angrier than he'd intended, and he winced internally as Sophie's knees buckled. Striding to her side, he eased her into the armchair. Her head didn't quite reach the top of his chest and her slight figure curved unconsciously into his body.

Damn if she didn't feel amazing in his arms.

Sophie stared up at him wordlessly, and he momentarily got lost in green eyes and long, thick eyelashes. Right before he mentally shook himself. Jesus, was he really attracted to his brother's fiancé? He needed to get a grip.

He was here to speak to his brother. The little shit wasn't answering his phone, but if he thought he could risk Robert's future on the farm and not expect a visit from his big brother, then he had another thing coming.

And as pretty as Sophie might be, no doubt she was elbow deep in the mess Damien was making.

The two brother's each owned half of the 7,000-acre property their parents had left them when they'd been killed in a car accident while the boys were still at boarding school, but only Robert had shouldered the responsibility of it. Damien had chosen to remain in Sydney and hadn't set foot on their land since the day after their parent's funeral, while Robert had given up his own dreams of a university education to keep the farm operating.

He hadn't been able to stomach the thought of land that had been in their family for three generations being sold. And besides, even with an agronomy degree under his belt, he'd been intending on returning home regardless.

Turns out he didn't need an agronomy degree to make a success of the enterprise. At the ripe old age of 28 he had a business many seasoned farmers were envious of. Which made the sting of Damien's underhand dealings cut deeper.

"Are you okay? What the hell was that guy doing here?"

"Looking for Damien." Her voice was small and she didn't make eye contact.

"Sophie, where is Damien?" he asked, crouching his large frame in front of the armchair. In the face of her continued silence, he placed a finger under her chin and gently forced her gaze to met his own. "I need to know. And from what I just witnessed, you need to know too."

"I don't know. I really don't," she all-but whispered. "Ever since we broke up he's been sketchy with communication, and then he sent a text saying he had to take off for a while and I haven't heard anything from him for over three weeks."

"I don't understand how you can't not know where he is," Robert ran a hand through his hair in frustration. "Hang on, you broke up? Last I heard you were getting married."

At this rate, the creases in his forehead were going to become permanent. He was as confused as hell and had to wonder how much truth was coming out of her pretty little mouth. Was this an act to cover up any involvement she had in Damien siphoning money from the farm's bank account?

"I told you, we're not together. It's not my job to keep tabs on him anymore. He's been spiraling out of control and I wanted out – he's not the same man he was. He emptied our bank account and now I'm being evicted and I don't know how I'm meant to move all my furniture, or even where I'm going to move it to… and the bread is mouldy," she finished tremulously, a tear sliding down her smooth cheek.

Ah hell. This was definitely not what Robert had anticipated.

Anything But Love

ABOUT THE AUTHOR

Jacqueline picked up her first Mills & Boon novel when she was 14, and fell head over heels in love with the romance of a happily-ever-after. *Sweet Valley High* just couldn't compete after she got hooked on dashing heroes and plucky heroines.

She has a Bachelor Degree in Print Journalism but, having always been tempted to embellish the facts of a story, decided she was more suited to writing works of fiction. She writes in between wrangling two daughters and my very own tall, handsome husband. *wink wink*

For more on Jacqueline, you can find her at:
 www.jacquelinehayley.com
www.instagram.com/jacquelinehayleyromance
www.twitter.com/JHromance
www.facebook.com/jacquelinehayleyromance

A note from Jacqueline...

Thank you for reading my book - it would be amazing if you could take the time to let me know your thoughts...

Not only will this let me know what you feel about my writing, but potential readers will also value your feedback.

If you have bought this book from Amazon you will already have an account that will enable you to review books that you have bought, or have been given as a gift.

If you purchased via iBooks, you can search for Anything But Love and leave your review under the 'Reviews' tab (you need to include a title in order to submit the review)

Goodreads is an excellent site for readers and you can sign in with Facebook or sign up with an email address. This gives you access to thousands of books, enables you to connect with readers of the genres you enjoy, and leave reviews on any books that you have read and feel you would like to offer constructive comments. www.goodreads.com

What will really help me in my future writing is to know some of the following in your review.
1   What did you like or dislike about the style of writing?
2   What did you enjoy about the plot?
3   How did you feel about the main characters?
4   What were your feelings when you finished the book?
5   Anything else that you feel it is important to mention for the benefit of other readers
6   Would you recommend the book to others?

Thank you so much for taking the time to leave a review.
xxx

www.ingramcontent.com/pod-product-compliance
Lightning Source LLC
Chambersburg PA
CBHW071520110726
47908CB00003B/905